WITHDRAWN

THE MEANEST GIRL

THE MEANEST GIRL

DEBORA ALLIE

A DEBORAH BRODIE BOOK

ROARING BROOK PRESS

NEW MILFORD, CONNECTICUT

A Deborah Brodie Book

Published by Roaring Brook Press

A division of Holtzbrinck Publishing Holdings Limited Partnership

143 West Street, New Milford Connecticut 06776

Library of Congress Cataloging-in-Publication Data

Allie, Debora.

The meanest girl / Debora Allie.–1st ed.

p. cm.

"A Deborah Brodie book."

Summary: Sixth-grader Alyssa Fontana, who thinks that her life is perfect, becomes the object of a practical joke which she blames on Hayden Martin, the new girl, who is tagged "the meanest girl in town."

ISBN 1-59643-014-1

[1. Cliques (Sociology)–Fiction.   2. Practical jokes–Fiction.

3. Friendship–Fiction.   4. Middle Schools–Fiction.   5. Schools–Fiction.]

I. Title.

PZ7.A42529Me 2005

[Fic]–dc22   2004017548

Roaring Brook Press books are available for special promotions and premiums. For details, contact: Director of Special Markets, Holtzbrinck Publishers.

Book design by Jennifer Browne

Printed in the United States of America

First edition June 2005

2   4   6   8   10   9   7   5   3   1

Dedicated to my Subject Matter Experts,
Mrs. Wojeski's and Mrs. VerGow's 2002–2003 sixth-grade
reading class at Maple Hill Middle School, Castleton,
New York; to Samantha Grimm, who was a great help
with the manuscript early on; to my son, Jason, the joy
of my life; to Deborah Brodie, my editor, who saw
the diamond in the rough draft and made it sparkle;
and to Bill Reiss, my agent, who never stopped believing.
You are the greatest. Er, I mean . . . You rock, man!
(Sweet!)

CONTENTS

1

AN ALMOST PERFECT LIFE

My name is Maria Alyssa Louisa Elena Fontana. In my family, they say names follow you like curses.

I live with my mom, Maria Elisa Louisa Theresa Fontana, in an apartment building in Brooklyn that used to be a shoe factory. I like to think about all those shoes—red pumps, brown loafers, pink fuzzy bunny slippers—riding on a conveyer belt through the nine stories of our building. Outside we have a courtyard and benches and birdbaths and the most grass you can find this side of Prospect Park, with a big black iron gate facing the bad neighborhood so no one can get in.

We live in Carroll Gardens, named after the only Roman Catholic signer of the Declaration of Independence, which my grandmother, Nonna, is very proud of and never lets me forget. Or that the movie *Moonstruck* was filmed here. Or that the Smith and Ninth Street stop of the F train is the highest stop in the whole subway system. (You can see the Statue of Liberty from there. Depending on where you stand on the platform, you might even be able to see the Empire State Building. I used to be able to see the World Trade Center.)

I go to P.S. 58, the Carroll School, and I used to have a perfect life. Well, almost perfect. Pretty good anyway—that is, until the meanest girl came to town. Hayden Martin is in the sixth grade like me. She moved here from Albany, the capital of New York, where the governor lives. She's the meanest girl in the whole school. They must grow them mean upstate.

Last week she put a huge wad of gum in my hair in math class. It was so bad I had to go to Aunt Elena's salon in Brooklyn Heights and have half my hair cut off.

The other day, she elbowed me in the stomach during gym. She made it look like she was guarding me, but I wasn't even trying to get the ball. I hate basketball.

But yesterday was the worst. I was standing at my locker talking to Dillon, and Hayden whipped up my skirt. I had pink underwear on! Dillon whistled and made all kinds of stupid boy noises. I was so embarrassed. I will *never* wear pink underwear ever again.

Yup, she's mean. Hayden Martin is just plain mean.

I don't know why she hates me so much. Maybe it's because I have shiny, straight black hair and hers is brown and frizzy. Maybe it's because she's short and chunky, and I am tall and thin. Maybe it's because Dillon Mahoney likes me and not her. Maybe it's because I get straight A's and she gets C's. I don't know why she doesn't like me, but she sure is mean.

At least I don't have to see her after school. We both live on Court Street, but she lives more toward Cobble Hill and I live more toward Red Hook. I don't go down that way except to take ballet lessons with Chelsea. (Some day we are going to be in the New York City Ballet together. Truly.)

"Alyssa! Lyss! Lyss!" Chelsea Gardner, my best friend since kindergarten, runs toward me as I put my books in my locker.

"Hey, Chels." Chelsea is one of the prettiest girls in school. She has the blondest, most beautiful hair you've ever seen and green eyes. And not only is she pretty, but she can do anything. Gymnastics. Show jumping. Ballet. She's the *perfect* ballerina. I'm lucky she's my friend.

"My party's tomorrow," she says. Like I don't know. Like she needs to remind me.

"Cool."

"Mom says this year we can stay up as late as we want to."

"No way!" *Awesome.*

* 3 *

On the way to the party, I'm thinking about my present for Chels. It will be her favorite. I just know it.

"Hey, Alyss!" Bri yells when I walk in the door.

I look around. Everyone's here . . . Nicole, Bri, Keila, Hayden . . . *Hayden*? *What*? What is *she* doing here?

I run into the kitchen and grab Chelsea by the arm. "What is Hayden doing here?"

"My mother said I had to invite her. Her mother works with my father. She told him that Hayden is having a hard time making friends at school."

"Duh!" Like, gee, what a surprise! I peek around the corner. Frizzhead is sitting in the corner of the living room, her present on her lap, staring into space. No one is talking to her. Oh, poor Hayden.

Yeah, right.

We have pizza, do the birthday-cake thing (Chelsea's mom actually made a cake that looks like Chelsea riding a horse), and then it's time for the presents. Chelsea opens mine first, pulling out a journal with a picture of a ballerina on the front.

"Oh, Alyss, I love it!" She takes off the key and opens it. "And two tickets to the New York City Ballet! Thanks, Lyss!" Chelsea runs over and hugs me. I am, after all, her *best friend.*

"We can go together," I suggest, being the unselfish person that I am.

* 4 *

Chelsea opens Hayden's gift last. "Oh . . . Oh my gosh. Thank you, Hayden." She holds up a Sony CD Walkman. I can't believe it. Mega gift. Mega bucks.

Hayden is looking at her feet, like she's embarrassed or something. She should be, trying to buy my best friend!

Well, she might have given Chelsea the best gift, but I'm still *Chelsea Gardner's best friend*, I think to myself, folding my arms across my chest. I am, and always will be, Chelsea's best friend.

2

TRUTH OR DARE

Makeover time. Chelsea's specialty.

Bri paints her fingernails and toenails white. Bri is the tallest girl in our class, with skin the color of chocolate and eyes the color of coal. She's one of the most beautiful girls I have ever seen.

I paint my nails red. Nicole paints hers pink. They come out all uneven and lumpy, kind of like Nicole herself. Nicole, despite her pretty name, is short, chubby, with dirty blond hair and wire-frame glasses. She's nice and all, but not really part of the "in" crowd. Not the sharpest tool in the shed, if you know what I mean. If smarts were a lightbulb, Nicole would be 40 watts. Chelsea likes her because, well, she is really nice, but mostly because they ride horses together upstate. Their families are both kind of rich.

Keila paints her fingernails and toenails black, in stark contrast to her pale white skin. Kei always looks cool. She dresses like a hip tomboy, wearing hip T-shirts and really funky jeans, and has short black hair that is longer on one side than on the other, real artsy-looking. Could be because her mom is the famous artist Marguerite Justice. Marguerite makes collages out of things that most people throw away. Broken, ugly things people throw away. I keep trying to see what is so great about her work, but it looks ugly to me, no matter how hard I try.

Chelsea paints hers orange. That's Chelsea for you. I think they invented orange just for her.

We paint our eyes, our cheeks, our lips. We are beautiful. Well, most of us.

"Hayden, can I do your hair?" Chelsea asks. Hayden looks unsure, but then she nods.

What!? Why is she being so nice to her?

"Let's go wet it under the sink," Chelsea says, pulling her into the kitchen.

Chelsea wets Hayden's hair, and suddenly, it turns curly. No more frizz. Then she puts gel in and scrunches it with her fingers. "Always use gel," Chelsea says, wagging her finger at Hayden. "And if you have to blow-dry it, use a diffuser. That way your hair won't frizz out." She hands Hayden a mirror.

Hayden just stares. Then a slow smile creeps across her face. Between the makeup and the new hair, she does look kind of good.

I think I'm going to throw up.

I think, maybe I should put gum in her hair, like she did to me. Let's see if gel can take care of that.

But then we put on our pajamas and dance, and I feel better.

And during the pillow fight, I hit Hayden really hard. And I feel even better.

By the time we have banana splits, I am in a great mood.

Then it's time to go to bed. We lay our sleeping bags on the floor. I'm trying to get mine next to Chelsea's like I always do, but Hayden is on one side and Nicole is on the other.

I cannot believe it. I always sleep next to Chelsea. Everyone knows this. It's an unwritten law, like gravity. Apples fall from trees, and I sleep next to Chelsea. That's just the way it is.

Clearly this is Hayden's doing and not Chelsea's. Clearly.

"So I hear you made out with Dillon behind the gym," Bri says, sitting up on one elbow, staring at me.

"I did not!" What is she doing?

"Ooh . . ." everyone says.

"We did not make out! We were only talking," I say, wishing they'd shut up.

"Well, Dillon told Zack, who told Donnell, who

told me that you made out," Bri says, pointing at me.

"In his dreams!" My face is on fire, I'm so embarrassed.

"Dillon's just trying to look good to his friends," Chelsea says. Everyone nods.

"He is pretty cute," Bri says. "I wouldn't mind kissing him myself." We all laugh. She's at least a foot taller then Dillon.

I jump on her, pretending I'm angry, starting the pillow fight all over again. We roll all over the floor, giggling.

"Seriously," Bri says. "Has anyone here ever kissed a boy? Alyss, *truth or dare!*"

She's starting to annoy me.

"No!"

"You're supposed to say 'truth.'"

Like *really* annoy me.

"Truth. I've never kissed a boy." Could we possibly change the subject?

"Okay, Alyssa, go ahead and pick someone," Bri says.

Ahh . . . sweet revenge. "Bri, truth or dare?"

"Truth."

"Have you ever kissed anyone?"

"Yes, my mama, every night," she says, falling on the floor, laughing.

"That doesn't count! That doesn't count!" we all yell and start hitting each other with pillows again.

"Okay, okay. Yes, I've kissed a boy."

Pillows drop to the floor, and everyone settles into a circle around Bri, like we're worshipping a goddess. Hayden practically sits on top of Chelsea. The weasel.

"Really?" someone says.

"Who?"

"What was it like?"

"Find out for yourself!" Bri yells, grabbing a pillow, trying to resume the fight.

"C'mon, tell us, tell us!" we all yell.

"Well, ya know Randy Johnson? R. J.?"

"R. J.! Oh my gosh, oh my gosh," we all say. Everyone knows R. J. He's *only* the star of the JV basketball team, and he's in *ninth grade.*

"Well, he's best friends with Donnell," Bri says. Donnell is Bri's older brother. "I've known him since we were little. I used to have a major crush on him. One day when I was in first grade and he was in fourth grade, he came over to our house. We were all just hanging out, and I kissed him right on the mouth!"

"Ahh!" we yell.

"That doesn't count!" Chelsea shouts.

"Does, too!" Bri yells back, laughing.

"Does not!" we all shout. "You were only six!"

"I'm just messing with ya," Bri says. "Me? Kiss a boy? Are you kidding? My mama would kill me! What do you think she keeps me in church and youth group all the time for? Besides," Bri says, flashing that huge smile of hers, "I've got to concentrate on my career."

Career! We are in sixth grade! *Career?*

"I'm going to do some modeling for a catalogue. And someday I might even be Miss America, to help pay for school. I'm going to be a doctor someday. A pediatrician, so I can take care of kids." Bri's little brother is sick all of the time. He has multiple sclerosis or muscular dystrophy or something. I can never remember which.

"Boring!" Chelsea yells. "I'd rather kiss a boy!"

"Eww!" everyone yells. Then we smash Chelsea in the face with pillows and pile on top of her.

"Okay, Bri, now you pick," Chelsea says. I hope she picks Hayden.

"Keila, truth, dare, or double dare!" Leave it to Bri to add the double dare. I'm glad she didn't pick me.

"Double dare!" Keila shouts.

Double dare! I can't believe it. She could get in major trouble with a double dare!

3

DOUBLE Dare!

Bri rubs her hands together and looks to the ceiling, trying to think up something good. All of a sudden, she jumps up and points at Kei. "You have to send someone a love letter!"

"Aah!" we all say, rolling around on the floor, laughing and making noises like we've just been punched in the stomach. Ugh!

Keila makes a sucking-in sound, like uh-oh, and covers her mouth with her hands.

"So, who's it going to be?" Bri asks, hands on her hips.

"Who's it going to be!" we all yell, jumping to our feet and wiggling back and forth, imitating Bri.

"Let me think," Kei says.

"Stop stalling," Bri says.

"Um . . . Anthony Pagano."

Anthony Pagano! Man, she's shooting for the top—Anthony is so cute!

"Don't you live by him?" Chelsea asks.

Keila nods.

"Uh-uh. No good," Bri says, waving her hand. "If it doesn't work out, you'll see him all the time, and then you'll be embarrassed. Seeing him at school would be bad enough. But you could see him on the subway, at the market. . . . Don't even think about it."

How does Bri know these things? She must learn this stuff from her older sisters or something.

Keila says, "I guess you're right."

"I'm right, girl," Bri says, waving a hand at her. "Trust me."

"But I don't like anybody else!"

"Pick somebody cute," suggests Chelsea.

"Yeah," says Hayden, nodding. Oh, like she knows anything.

"Or somebody you'd like to know," Nicole says.

"Yeah," Hayden says again.

I can't believe it! She'll do anything to fit in! She'll do anything to steal my friends! Can't they see that?

"Okay, I kind of like Jason Andrews," Keila says.

Jason Andrews! Jason Andrews! *I* have a crush on Jason Andrews. He is *so cute.* Blond hair, big blue eyes . . . not Jason Andrews!

"Actually, I heard that he's not very nice," I say innocently.

"Yeah, I heard that, too," Bri says, backing me up. Bri knows I've liked Jason since first grade. Even though I am sort of going out with Dillon Mahoney. Well, okay, I *am* going out with him. I like Dillon, but I'm not sure I *like* him like him. I don't think I'm *in love* or anything. It's just that he's the first guy to ever ask me out, so I said yes. All it really means is he stops by my locker sometimes and walks me to classes and stuff. Big deal. But still, it's nice to be able to say I have a boyfriend. (As long as I don't say it to my mother. She would *freak*.)

"What about Josh Martinez?" Bri says.

"Oooh," we all say. He's really cute, too. Dark-skinned, jet-black hair, big brown eyes.

"But what if he doesn't like me?" Keila asks.

"Too bad, Miss I'll-Take-the-Double-Dare!" Bri says.

Keila braces herself like she's facing a firing squad, then sits down to write her first love letter.

With a little help from her friends, of course.

It takes us *ten minutes* just to decide what paper she should use. Chelsea doesn't have any stationery with hearts on it. Keila was relieved about that. I can tell by the way she keeps taking deep breaths that she's pretty nervous about writing a love note to a cute boy she barely knows. Finally we select Chelsea's flowered note-paper, which is orange and pink, just like everything else she owns.

We huddle on Chelsea's bed, Hayden weaseling her way in next to Chelsea, while Keila sits at Chelsea's desk, writing with this huge pencil with a Tweety Bird eraser on top. It looks kind of dumb, but funny, too. After about a minute, we gather around her, looking over her shoulder.

"Stop standing over me!" she says. "I'll show it to you when I'm done."

She starts writing again, then balls up the note and throws it on the floor.

"Hey! That's good paper!" Chelsea says.

"Well, maybe you'd better give me practice paper!" Keila says. She sounds a little tense.

Chelsea practically runs Nicole down to hand Keila notebook paper before any more of her good stationery is ruined.

Keila starts writing, then crumples up what she's written. She starts writing again, then crumples it up again. Balled-up pieces of paper cover the floor. Finally she finishes, places Tweety down on the desk, and sighs.

"Read it!" we all yell.

Dear Josh,
    You probably don't know me. My name
is Keila Justice, and I'm in study hall with
you. (I sit at the table in the back corner

with Anna Jankowski.) I'm the one with the funky black hair.

I like to play basketball and watch it on TV. My favorite team is the Knicks (kind of obvious, I know), and my favorite ice cream is Mud over the Hudson, which they make at the store down the street from my house. I also love pizza, and I'm the family Ping-Pong queen.

I was wondering if you like me. If you do, please wear a blue-and-yellow shirt on Wednesday the 17th.

Keila Justice

"I like it," Chelsea says.

"Me, too," Hayden gushes. The suck-up.

"Good idea about the shirt," Chelsea says.

"Yeah," Hayden agrees.

"Wait . . . don't you think it should say 'Love, Keila'?" Bri asks.

After a shout of unanimous agreement, Keila copies the wording onto the good paper, and puts "Love, Keila Justice" at the end. She looks kind of sick, like her dog has just been hit by a car. If she had a dog.

"Okay, what's his address?" Chelsea asks, holding up an envelope.

No one knows, so Chelsea gets the phone book and flips to the *Ms*. "There's a million Martinezes in this book! Anyone know where he lives?"

"President Street," Bri says.

"And you would know that *because*?" I whisper.

"I just know," she whispers back.

Hmmm . . .

Keila carefully folds the note and sticks it in the envelope. Then she copies the address from the phone book.

"You forgot to put your name and address in the corner," Hayden points out.

Wow, Hayden has an original thought!

Kei writes her return address in the corner and seals it, and Bri sticks on the stamp.

"We'll mail it in the morning," Chelsea says. "I'll sleep with it under my pillow . . . just to make sure it's safe."

We all laugh and head back to the living room for the rest of the night. I'm having a great time.

Until Hayden elbows me in the face.

4

Friends and Other Traitors

"Ow!" I yell, covering my eye with my hand.

"Oh, Lyss, I'm sorry," Hayden says.

"That's 'Alyssa,' to you."

"I didn't mean to hit you, I was trying to get up and—"

"Oh, yeah, right. Just like gym class."

"Knock it off, Alyssa," Chelsea says.

Knock it off! Knock it off! *What?* Whose side is she on?

Chelsea pulls my hand away from my eye like she's a nurse or something. "I'll get some ice."

I glare at Hayden.

"It's because she likes Dillon," I hiss to Bri.

"Shh . . . ," she says. "She'll hear you."

"I don't care!"

Everyone is staring at me. What?

Chelsea walks back in with the ice. "My mom says it's 'probably time to calm down.'" We climb into our sleeping bags.

My sleeping bag is *so embarrassing.* Aunt Louisa gave it to me for my birthday and it looks like it belongs to a five-year-old. It has huge pink-and-yellow flowers on it.

Hayden's sleeping bag is big and gray and sporty-looking. She looks like she could sleep on Mt. Everest in that thing. Maybe I could arrange that . . . a nice, cold hike up Mt. Everest, never to return. She is, after all, *ruining my life.* Beating me up, sticking gum in my hair, stealing my friends . . .

"Lyss, do you really think Bri will be Miss America?" Nicole whispers to me.

"What?"

"Do you really think Bri will be Miss America someday?"

"I dunno," I say, readjusting the bag of ice. I can't believe Hayden elbowed me in the eye. I know she did it on purpose.

"Which state would she be?" Nicole asks.

"What?"

"Which state would she be if she were in the Miss America pageant?"

She's serious. *Duh!*

"Well, Nick, I suppose if she's from New York, she would represent New York State."

"Oh."

I wish she'd leave me alone. Can't she tell I'm not

exactly in a good mood? Can't she see I just want to sit here and feel sorry for myself, like any self-respecting person who has just been elbowed in the eye by the meanest girl in school?

"What do you want to be when you grow up?" Nicole asks.

"I don't know, Nick! I'm in sixth grade! How am I supposed to know what I want to be when I grow up?"

"I want to be a teacher," Nicole says.

Well, that's real original there, Nicole. It's the only job that we see on a day-to-day basis.

"I want to work with kids who have a hard time learning."

"I want to work with pygmies in Africa," I say sarcastically.

"What are they like?" Nicole asks.

"Who?"

"The pygmies in Africa."

"I'm only kidding, Nick. I don't even know if there *are* pygmies in Africa. I don't even know what a pygmy is. Bri was telling me the other day about these people from her church who are missionaries who go to Africa to help poor people, and it just popped into my head. I was just fooling around."

"Oh," Nicole says, embarrassed.

I turn over on my side. The floor is so hard. I look at Hayden, all comfortable in her puffy sleeping bag, sleeping right next to my best friend. I think bad things, like maybe I should cut off all her hair while she's sleeping, or maybe I should pour water in her sleeping bag and everyone will think she peed.

But I'm not that mean, which really annoys me. Hayden would do that, but not me.

The next morning, we all walk outside with Keila to the mailbox and mail the love note. Keila is about to drop it in, when Chelsea slaps her hand away.

Oh, here we go. Chelsea has decided to make a ceremony out of the whole thing. Can't we just get on with it?

"What?" Kei asks, annoyed. I don't blame her.

"I think we should say something special," Chelsea says, "something to always remember this day. To love and double dares!" she shouts dramatically, one arm in the air.

Bri and I roll our eyes at each other.

"Come on, you guys!" she says. "To love and double dares!"

"To love and double dares!" we all shout so we can go back into the house, since we are, after all, standing in the street in our pajamas.

Chelsea pulls back the handle of the mailbox and Kei drops in the letter.

"Last one in the house has to kiss Jason Andrews!" Bri yells, like this is a bad thing. But we try to outrun each other anyway.

We get dressed, and then it's time to eat. Mrs. G. has outdone herself as usual. She's made pancakes, blueberry muffins, scrambled eggs, bacon, and sausage. She lives for this stuff. She's so weird, like she's from the 1950s or something. She wears dresses, and sometimes even an apron. She always looks like she just stepped out of a salon, her blond hair falling to her shoulders, straight and smooth, her face always perfectly made up. She uses words like "lady" and "proper." She bakes orange cupcakes for Halloween, green ones for St. Patrick's Day, purple ones for Easter. She's nothing at all like my mom.

So we're eating this beautiful breakfast in the Gardners' beautiful dining room when, all of a sudden, Nicole starts coughing and orange juice comes out of her nose!

"Eww!"

"Awwh!"

"Gross!"

Our heads are on the table, we are laughing so hard.

Well, except for Nicole, who looks kind of pale. Then she starts laughing, too.

I give her credit. You've got to be brave to laugh at yourself when you do something embarrassing in front of people.

As we are eating, everyone's mom starts to show up. Bri's, who is tall and beautiful, just like Bri. Kei's, who is short and pale, just like Kei. (We all yell "Josh" in a singsong kind of way as she leaves.) Nicole's dad. Everyone—except my mom and Hayden's.

Mrs. G. sticks her head into the living room. "Alyssa, your mom's going to be a little late."

Great. I'm stuck here with Frizzhead. I get up and drag Chelsea into the kitchen.

"What are you doing?" I ask.

"What?"

"You are being so nice to Hayden. What, is she your best friend now?"

"No, but I have to be nice to her. My mom said so. Anyway, she's not that bad."

Not that bad. Not that bad. *Right.*

I plop myself on the living room couch and cross my arms across my chest. Hayden stares at her feet. Then, thank the Blessed Virgin, the doorbell rings. My mother is at the door, and it's time to leave.

I grab my things and stand up. Hayden doesn't look up.

"Hayden, honey, is your mom coming?" Chelsea's mom asks.

"I don't know," she says.

"Do you want to call her?"

"I already did. She's not home and she's not answering her cell phone. She's probably at work."

"On Saturday?"

Hayden nods. "She works a lot. She's a lawyer."

"What about your dad?" I ask.

Chelsea's mom glares at me. What? I'm just trying to be helpful.

"Well, I don't know what to do," Chelsea's mom says. "We have to leave in a few minutes to go upstate. We have a one o'clock luncheon with Chelsea's grandmother."

And then I hear the words that will haunt me for a lifetime.

"She can come home with us," my mother says.

"No!" I yell, glaring at my mother. "I mean, Mom, don't we have . . . don't we have that thing we have to do?"

"What thing?" she says, looking at me, confused.

Then Mom says to Hayden, "Leave a message for

your mom that you will be at our house." She gives her our phone number.

It's a nightmare. An absolute nightmare!

Hayden Martin, the meanest girl in school, is coming to my house.

5

MELTDOWN ON COURT STREET

As we walk toward our building, suddenly I'm not so psyched that we live in a renovated shoe factory that used to have red heels and fuzzy pink bunny slippers traveling through it on conveyor belts. I wish I lived in a brownstone like Chelsea. I'm wondering what Hayden is going to think, and I'm afraid that that my uncle Dominic, my mom's younger brother and the baby of the family (even though he's twenty-eight), will be hanging out his front window like he always is, wearing a sleeveless white undershirt with a stain on it, telling whoever passes by about his heartburn, his blood pressure, the weather, and his mother, my grandmother, Maria Louisa Theresa Mary Feraco. Nonna.

They say at church that God made Heaven and Earth, but it's hard to believe Nonna didn't have something to do with it. Nonna brought five girls and one boy into this world and she'll never let you forget it. Or that she raised them on her own. Or about the curse.

Always, we hear about the evil eye, the curse. Everyone in our family has been touched by the curse, according to Nonna. I'd always thought I had escaped it. But now it looks like the evil eye has got me, too . . . in the form of Hayden Frizzhead Martin!

As we round the corner, I see just what I have feared: Uncle Dom hanging out his window in his white tank top, feeding the pigeons last night's pizza crust.

Mom yells at him to stop, like she always does. He keeps throwing stuff, like he always does. Mom yells back that he's responsible for half the roaches in Brooklyn. He says something about her hair.

Is there a hole I can fall into?

I stomp into the building and push the buzzer. Stanley the doorman lets us in. Well, at least we have a doorman. That ought to impress Hayden.

I love Stanley. He always says hi to me and makes me feel good, like I'm special or something. He says stuff like, "How's my girl doin'?" and "Why, Miss Alyssa, don't you look fine today."

We take the elevator to the fifth floor. When Mom opens the door, I look around our apartment with new eyes—Hayden eyes. What will she think of our apartment? What will she tell everyone at school? It's not exactly a brownstone like Chelsea has.

Our dining room, living room, and kitchen are one big room. The windows in all of the rooms are huge, and we have hardwood floors. Not the nice hardwood floors that are shiny and perfect like at Chelsea's house, but the kind with paint spots and dark marks here and there. My mom calls it the "natural look."

Our dining room is a wooden table that leans against the wall between the bedrooms. The kitchen has a different kind of floor so that you can pretend it's a separate room. On the other side of the kitchen wall lives a guy who speaks French, is really mean, and plays his music way too loud.

Mom's room is covered floor to ceiling with books on psychology, nature, art, and other stuff. And there are a bunch she saved for me that she read when she was young—Nancy Drew, the Hardy Boys, and Trixie Belden, my favorite. Mom says Trixie has a cult following. Even though the author is dead, people, regular people (not real writers), are still writing the books and putting them on the Internet. I think that is so cool.

In the corner of Mom's office (not in the living room where normal people would put it) stands a small television, for the few times I'm allowed to watch TV. We don't even have cable, just one of those dorky antennas. Wait until Hayden sees that. Why do we have to be so weird about everything?

I go to my room and slam the door, leaving Hayden and Mom alone in the living room.

Mom barges into my room. "Why are you being so rude?"

"Mom," I say, pointing out the door, "that's Hayden Martin!"

"So!"

"She's the one who stuck the gum in my hair!" I say, tossing my hair from side to side, like, *hello,* this is why I have short hair now.

"Well . . . well . . . it's time for lunch."

"I'm not hungry!" I fold my arms across my chest and stare at the floor.

"Eat anyway," she says, marching out of my room.

Doesn't she care? Doesn't she care at all? I mean, I did have to get my hair cut off!

That's it. I'm not eating. And then it hits me. *Oh, no!*

I run into the kitchen. "Why don't we order pizza?" I suggest.

But it's too late. Mom is already pulling food out of the fridge: hummus (roasted red pepper), hummus (forty spices, for some variety), bean sprouts, the green stuff, portabello mushrooms, the orange stuff, salad, cheese made from vegetables instead of milk, the yellow stuff. . . .

I plop down in the chair and sigh, holding my head

in my hands. Why can't she be like other people's moms? Why can't we eat normal food, like peanut butter and jelly?

"Oh, hummus, I love hummus," Hayden says, smearing some orange stuff on a pita. Figures. *Suck-up.*

"How long have you lived in Brooklyn?" Mom asks.

"Not long. We just moved here from Albany a few months ago."

"Albany? Really? Do you know the Panessas?" Mom asks, excited.

Hayden shakes her head.

Like Albany is a small town. *Duh.* It *is* the capital!

I push some bean sprouts and some veggie cheese into a pita. No way am I eating hummus. ("But it's made of chickpeas!" Mom says. Oh, like that would change my mind.)

At least there's salad. I pick out a handful of croutons and line them up in front of me, ready for flicking.

"What is Albany like?" Mom asks.

"Quieter. Much quieter than here. And you don't have to drive far to be in the country, which is really pretty."

"And your father, where does he work?"

"Don't know. He left a year ago. Haven't heard from him." Hayden looks down at her plate and I think, Oh, poor Hayden. *Right.*

I flick a crouton in her direction. It bounces off the salad bowl. No one notices. Mom and Hayden are deep in conversation.

"I'm sorry, sweetie. Life can be hard sometimes," Mom says. "We know a little about that," she says, looking around the apartment.

"My father died in a motorcycle accident on the BQE when I was one," I explain. Which is a lot worse than somebody taking off when you're twelve.

Suddenly everyone is very quiet. Then Hayden says, "Oh. Sorry, Alyssa."

I feel victorious, my tragedy being worse than hers, until I look at my mother, who is sinking down into her chair like she wants to hide.

"What?" I say.

"Nothing," Mom says.

"No! What?"

"*Nothing*. We'll talk about it later, Alyssa."

It? It? What's *it*?

Mom looks guilty, like she's done something wrong, and I'm starting to get a really bad feeling.

She doesn't say anything.

"But he died in an accident."

Mom shakes her head and starts toward me.

"No! Don't touch me!"

All of my life, no one has ever wanted to talk about my father. But now I know the truth.

He left us. Just like Frizzhead's father.

I run into my room, lock the door, and throw myself on my bed.

Does he have another family that he loves more than us?

I can't believe Hayden is in my apartment right now! Why doesn't she go home! I want to scream, punch something. My throat hurts from trying not to cry.

I punch my pillow over and over, and try to forget the world around me, try to forget that Hayden Martin, the meanest girl in school, just saw me have a meltdown, an absolute meltdown, and will probably tell the whole school that I didn't even know my father left us.

Left me.

6

MEAN, GREEN SALES QUEEN

The next morning, Mom tries to talk to me, but I totally ignore her. I hate her right now. Absolutely hate her.
I grab a box of cereal, walk back to my room, and slam
the door.

I eat almost three bowls, then start reading book
number 20 of the Trixie Belden series, *The Mystery of Old
Telegraph Road*. But I can't concentrate. Who cares about
Trixie Belden right now? I turn on my radio and flop
into my beanbag chair.

Mom knocks on the door.

I pretend I don't hear.

"Alyssa."

Not hearing . . .

She opens the door. The nerve! I fold my arms across
my chest and swivel around so my back is to her.

She sighs. "Get dressed. We're going shopping."

"I don't want to go shopping."

"Well, we're going, so get dressed."

"Why can't I stay here?"

"Because I said . . . Because I want you to go shopping with me."

Right. Like she cares about me. She knows I hate to shop. And it's not like I don't know what's really going on.

Mom always goes shopping when she's upset about something. Like pants or a new shirt will fix all her problems. Hah! The shrink needs retail therapy. How pathetic is that?

Just to annoy her, I put on my favorite pants, the black-and-gray checked ones with the drawstring top that she considers pajama pants and I consider perfectly-fine-for-going-out pants.

She grabs her purse and keys, takes one look at me, and starts to say, "You're not going out in . . ." Then sighs and stops.

Ha.

We walk out the door. The elevator *ding*s, and Mom pushes *L*. *L* as in lobby, *L* as in loser, *L* as in lousy day. *L* as in I am *livid*.

We cross the street, and Mom takes the fliers off our car, a rusty, pale yellow Volkswagen Bug that's always dirty because we hardly ever use it. She sprays Windex on the windshield and rubs a circle on the driver's side. She's just about finished, when a sparrow lands on the hood. Mom brushes him away, afraid he'll poop. He flies back. She shoos him away again. He flies back. She sprays him with Windex. Well, that ought to kill him. She's so mean!

He flies away. We get in, put on our seat belts, and, *as always,* Mom backs into the car behind us—her wonderful technique for getting out of tight parking spots. She pulls forward, backs up again, cranks the wheel to the left, pulls up a little, backs up again, then finally gets out of the spot. I shrink down in my seat. Could she be any more embarrassing?

We drive to the gas station, and *as usual,* Mom forgets which side of the car the gas tank is on. And, *as usual,* she forgets to pay before she pumps. So she stands there, wiggling and jiggling the pump handle and wondering why nothing is coming out, until I remind her—*duh,* like *hello!*—"Pay before you pump!"

I guess she has a lot on her mind. Regular unleaded versus premium. Cash versus credit. When she last checked the oil. When she was planning to tell me my father is alive.

And then we are on our way, Mom, me, and lemon-scented John Lennon swinging from the mirror.

Oh, yay.

We drive through the Battery Tunnel and up FDR Drive. We're probably going to Bloomingdale's, Mom's favorite store, but I don't ask.

I'm probably the only girl in the world who hates to shop. Well, except for Kei. She hates to shop, too, which might be why she looks the way she does sometimes. I think she even wears her brother's jeans, because they always look big and she wears a big belt. She gets away with it, though, because everyone thinks of her as the artistic type, like her mother.

"I thought we'd get you a bra today," Mom says, like it's just an ordinary shopping trip. Like it's not my first bra. Like this is supposed to be some kind of treat.

I sling my seat belt across my flat chest. Yeah, like I really need a bra. Right. Right-o, mama-o.

I watch the river go by and try to prepare myself for what is to come. My mom will make getting my first bra into a big thing. She's probably already called PBS to make a documentary about it. ("Join us today while Alyssa Fontana buys her first bra.") Worst of all, she will say "breasts" over and over again, because she always insists on using the proper word for all body parts. "Boobs" will not do. I'm glad I'm not a boy!

And so, to shield myself from the embarrassment and sheer humiliation that is to come, I throw my mind into a parallel universe where we are not bra shopping, and the woman driving the beat-up Volkswagen is not my mother. In fact, we are tooling around in a big red convertible, not a VW; my mother is someone cool, not, well, who she is; and we are driving across the country to escape from ugly men who want nothing more than to dance with the two most beautiful women they have ever seen. We are tough, we are beautiful, and we have very, very big boobs.

The saleswoman at Bloomingdale's looks like an Iraqi tank. She's huge and wears a dark green suit with a yellow-red-and-green scarf tied just right. I think she must have gone to school to learn how to tie that scarf. I wonder if she has a degree in scarf tying.

She also has a mole the size of Staten Island growing out of her face. With a hair sticking out of it. Ugh! Like, *tweezers, hello*!

She wastes no time when she sees us. "Can I help you?" she asks, giving us both the up-and-down look, and making me feel small.

"My daughter is buying her first bra today," Mom says, putting her arm around my shoulder, like she's proud of me or something. I don't know why she's so proud of me, it was bound to happen someday, and I am, after all, flat as a board. I squirm away.

"So you need a brassiere," the saleswoman says, her voice booming. I want to disappear.

"What size do you think you need?" she says, staring at my chest. I have the horrible thought that she's going to reach out and tweak me.

Mom says, "I think you could help us with that. Her breasts"—There it is, I think, the word. She just had to say it the proper way—"are kind of on the small side."

Is there a hole in the floor I can fall into?

"Ah, yes," the woman says, looking me up and down again. "Let me get my tape."

Her *tape*! I glare at Mom. She is *not* going to measure my boobs!

Mean, Green Sales Queen reaches for the shelf under the cash register and pulls out a measuring tape like you use to measure the width of windows, the length of a skirt, but not my boobs. I back away.

Mom catches on (finally) and says, "I don't think that will be necessary. Why don't you just point us in the right direction?"

We follow Freaky Sales Queen as she walks toward a display of very small bras. Something about her doesn't look right, like the fact that she has shoulders the size of a football player's. I'm starting to think that she's not a woman at all, but a man dressed as a woman.

"These are good starter bras," she says, waving a hand. "You are probably a thirty-two triple A." She pulls out a pink bra with little butterflies on the cups. I shake my head. I hate pink. Too girly-girly. No way.

"No? How about this?" She holds up a shiny black bra.

I nod.

Mom says, "Too sexy. I can't believe they even make that for young girls. I'll take it from here. Thank you for your time."

"Well, let me know if you need any help, and don't forget the matching panties!" Sales Queen's voice booms across the store. Great. How many people in Manhattan now know I am buying a AAA bra with matching panties?

Mom picks through the selection. I stand in the aisle with my arms folded across my chest.

"How about this?" Mom says, holding up a bra that looks like a miniature tank top. It's white and sporty-looking.

"Okay," I say.

"Let's get a few different kinds to see what is most comfortable."

We end up buying two of the sporty tank top kind, one plain white and one with some yellow trim. Mom says that if I get red or blue, it will show through my shirt—yikes. I don't even want anyone to know I'm wearing a bra. Mom lets me buy the matching underwear, even though she says they are "kind of skimpy."

"I'm glad you got the panties." The Saleswoman from Hell's voice booms through the store. I can't decide whether to crawl under the cash register or punch her in the nose.

Both. I want to do both.

Finally, we get all my stuff into the bag, where no one can see it.

"How about some lunch?" Mom asks, apparently still not wanting to go home. "The Hard Rock Café is not too far from here."

I shrug, like I don't care, but secretly I'm kind of psyched. Chelsea says the Hard Rock is pretty cool.

7
MELTDOWN AT THE HARD ROCK

On the way to lunch, I see a man holding a little girl's hand, a father with his daughter, the way things should be, which makes me even angrier. So, right there on the corner of Fifty-seventh Street and Broadway, I have my second meltdown.

"How could you?" I scream, arms waving.

"What?" Mom says, *as if she doesn't know.*

"Why didn't you tell me about my father?" I say, tears streaming down my cheeks.

"Oh, honey," Mom says. She pulls me to the side of a building and reaches to hug me.

"Don't," I say, pushing her away.

"It's not what you think," she says, with a pleading look on her face. Her eyes are wet but not overflowing like mine.

"How do you know what I think!" I yell, and this time the tears come really hard. I wipe them with the back of my hand. "You never know what I think!"

"You were just one when your dad left," she says. "For a long time, you didn't mention or ask about him, and I was relieved. I didn't say anything about it."

I start to say, "You should have—" but I'm feeling dazed and exhausted, so I just stare at the sidewalk. A little brown bird hops near my foot. I shoo it away.

At the Hard Rock, the back end of an old car from the 1950s or 1960s or something sticks out the front of the building, which is kind of cool, but I could hardly care, I'm so tired.

Guitars, clothes, and gold albums hang on the walls. Televisions everywhere play music videos. Loud music videos—too loud, when I feel this tired.

The hostess says there are no tables. Mom asks if we can sit at the bar.

"Okay with you?" Mom asks. Whatever.

"Why didn't you tell me the truth about my father?" I need to know.

Just as she's about to answer, the bartender comes over. He's wearing a black T-shirt, black jeans, and black boots. He has brown hair pulled back in a ponytail and dark skin like mine. Bulging muscles stick out from under his shirt.

I'm starting to feel a little better.

Mom orders a margarita, frozen, with salt.

"I'll have one of those," I say.

The cute bartender laughs. Mom says, "It's got tequila in it, hon. Why don't you try something else?"

Argh. How embarrassing. I order a root beer float.

"One margarita and one root beer float coming up," Hunky Bartender says. His nametag says his name is Jon. He's so dark-skinned, I think he looks more like a Juan or Julio or something. Like Johnny Depp in *Don Juan DeMarco* (Mom's favorite shrink movie), but darker and cuter. I decide to think of him as Jon Juan Bartendo.

"Why didn't you tell me the truth?" I ask as soon as he leaves.

"I was afraid you'd feel rejected, that he didn't love you."

Well, I guess he *didn't* love me, since he left!

"So I didn't say anything. I'm sorry. I should have told you."

I stare at the menu, pretending to read, too upset to see. And then Jon Juan is back with our drinks.

"Ready to order, ladies?" he asks, flashing the whitest teeth I have ever seen.

"We'll need another minute," Mom says. She runs a hand through my hair. "I didn't want you to be hurt, honey. And I wanted to tell you. As you got older, I wanted and planned to tell you the truth. But the older you got, the harder it was to talk to you about it. And you've been so happy and well adjusted. I didn't want to mess that up. I didn't want you to feel rejected, even though it was never about rejecting you. It wasn't even so much about rejecting me as much as it was about him being selfish."

Whenever I thought about my father, I've had a bad feeling, like something isn't right. Quiet thoughts would come and go, then slip away before I could dwell on them too long. Thoughts so uncomfortable they sprouted wings and flew away for months at a time.

"I had this feeling," I say, while I check out the menu.

"What?"

"You acted funny whenever I asked about him. I started to wonder."

"If he was alive?"

I nod, and hold my root beer float to my face. The frozen glass feels so good.

Jon Juan returns. "I'll have the Hard Rock Caesar Salad," Mom says.

"I'll have the Ringo Combo," I say.

"Coming right up," Jon says. His fingers touch mine as he reaches for the menu.

"Probably named after Ringo Starr," Mom says.

"What?"

"The Ringo Combo. It's probably named after Ringo Starr, one of The Beatles," Mom says.

I roll my eyeballs. I do *not* understand what the *big deal* is about The Beatles.

Mom points to a guitar on the wall. All I'm thinking about is Jon Juan Bartendo. His dark eyes, his white teeth. It's more fun than thinking about my father. It's more fun than thinking about how empty I feel inside.

"You know how the whole guitar-on-the-wall-thing at the Hard Rock started? Eric Clapton was a regular customer at the Hard Rock Café in London. Do you know who he is?"

"I think so. Isn't he the one whose little boy died and he wrote a song about it?"

"Yup. Well, anyway, Eric Clapton asked the bartender if he could hang his guitar on the wall to mark his favorite bar stool as his spot."

"And they let him?"

"Yup, and then a week later, Pete Townshend sent a guitar to the restaurant with a note saying his guitar was just as good as Clapton's, and he wanted his hung up, too. And that's how the whole thing started."

"Who's Pete Townshend?"

Mom sighs. "Oh, never mind."

Whatever.

And then suddenly he appears, Jon Juan Bartendo, bar hunk.

"Big day out today?" he asks. He's standing sideways, one elbow leaning on the bar. I can't take my eyes off him and his big white smile.

"We came into the city to do some shopping," Mom says.

"Buy anything good?"

"Nothing we can tell you about," I say.

"Aha," he says, turning toward me, resting both arms on the bar now. "And why is that?" He leans in close. I can smell his cologne.

"I could tell you, but then I'd have to kill you." It's something my sort-of-boyfriend Dillon always says.

"What, have you been shopping at Victoria's Secret?" Jon Juan asks, raising his eyebrows and turning to look at Mom.

"Something like that," she says, raising her chin, meeting his eyes. She traces her finger around the salt on the rim of her glass, licks her finger, meets his eyes again.

Is she flirting? *Gross!* I stare at her, dumbfounded. She'd better not be flirting! She's my mother. She's not supposed to flirt!

A young couple walks up to the end of the bar, and

Jon leaves. The guy has a hoop earring in each ear and really short blond hair. The girl has long, shiny blond hair, a dark tan, and her belly button pierced. He has his arm around her very thin waist. They both have tattoos and wear black jeans and boots.

My first thought is that they are beautiful. And then I look closer. They're in style, they're good-looking, but they look kind of trashy, too.

"Don't even think about it," Mom says.

"What?"

"The belly-button ring. Don't even think about it."

"I don't like belly-button rings."

"You don't?"

"Nope. Or tattoos. Remember the tattoos we saw at Jones Beach?" At Jones Beach, we had seen people with tattoos from the tops of their thighs all the way down to their ankles. It was disgusting. My mom has always told me to stay true to myself, even if it means being different. Now it's different *not* to have a tattoo.

"That's good. One battle down, twelve hundred left to go," Mom says, smiling.

"Mom, do you think Jon is cute?"

"Who?"

"The waiter. Do you think he's cute?"

"*Way* cute." She laughs.

Whoa. Mom notices guys. Gross me out.

"As cute as Dad?" I ask.

"In a different way," Mom says. She plays with the straw in her drink.

"So where is he?" I ask, staring at the bottom of my root beer float.

"Los Angeles. Where unhappy people go," Mom says.

"What?"

"Nothing." She waves her hand. "Some people think moving to a place where it's warm and sunny all the time will make them happy. But they bring themselves with them when they move, so nothing really changes. Forget about him, honey."

Forget about him! Forget about him! How can you forget your father! It's like having a leg amputated and trying not to feel the pain where it used to be.

I'm so angry I turn away, not wanting Mom to see my eyes, to see inside me.

I think, she just doesn't get it.

And, I hate him.

And, I wish he were dead.

And then I cry. Mom puts her arm around me. Jon brings another margarita without even asking, I have dessert, and we drive back to Brooklyn in silence.

When we get home, Mom puts on one of her old

Elton John albums. We are the only people in the world I know who don't have a CD player.

She puts on "Goodbye Yellow Brick Road," which, like the rest of E. J.'s songs, I don't understand but like. (It reminds me of the *Wizard of Oz*.) Then we put on his *Greatest Hits* album and dance to "Crocodile Rock." Mom does the twist and a dance where she looks like she's swimming and plugging her nose to go underwater. She's so corny! It makes me feel a little better.

Then we listen to Mom's absolute favorite Elton John song, "Mona Lisas and Mad Hatters." I've heard it so much I know the words. We belt it out, singing at the top of our lungs. The French guy next door starts banging on the walls because we're singing too loud. Too bad, the jerk. He's always loud!

I go to bed with visions of Jon Juan Bartendo dancing in my head.

8

CHELSEA GARDNER, PRESIDENT OF THE WORLD

I head straight for Chelsea's locker when I get to school on Monday. I want to tell her about what happened when Hayden came to my house, about my dad, bra shopping, Jon Juan. What a weekend!

"Chels, I'm so glad to see you. I *really* need to talk to you," I say.

Chelsea pulls books out of her locker. Everything inside her locker is orange and pink. "Oh, hey, Alyss," she says, without even turning around.

"Anyway, major stuff happened this weekend—"

"I'm glad you came by. I'm starting this club, and I know you'll want to be in it."

Great. "But—"

"All the most popular girls in the sixth grade will be in our club . . . you, me, Bri . . . I'm going to be president," Chelsea says.

She isn't listening to me at all. "Chels—"

"There's a meeting today at my house. Right after school. Can you come?" She closes her locker.

"Sure," I say. "Sure. I'm there." I watch her walk away.

I wanted to talk to her but she didn't care, so I just stand there, alone, books clutched to my chest, feeling like I'm going to cry.

And then I have the most terrible, horrible thought— did she invite Hayden to the meeting?

When I get to Chelsea's house, Mrs. Gardner is ironing and watching Oprah as usual. I say hi, even though I don't feel like it, and walk down the hall to Chelsea's room, which is pink and orange, just like her locker. Pink walls, orange bedspread. Pink pillows. Stuffed animals everywhere. Posters of horses, boys, and ballerinas.

I scan the room quickly. Bri, Nicole, Keila . . . no Hayden, thank God.

"Will the first meeting come to order!" Chelsea sits at her desk, banging her hair brush like a judge banging a gavel. Who does she think she is?

"Do you know what this is about?" I whisper to Bri.

"Nope," Bri says, shaking her head. "I thought you knew."

Nicole looks at me, confused. I shrug my shoulders.

"I have brought you all here today for a special meeting," Chelsea announces. "I feel that, in these difficult times, we must come together as sisters—"

Is she joking?

Bri has had enough already. "Chelsea, will you knock it off? You've been watching too much C-SPAN," she says. C-SPAN is on channel 3, the station you have to put on to watch a video, so we know a lot about C-SPAN.

"Brianna Loy Johnston . . ."

"Loy?" I whisper to Bri.

"My mother's maiden name," she mumbles. "I told her once. How she remembered it, I don't know."

She's like a politician, I think. Like on C-SPAN. She remembers everything so she can use it later.

Now where'd that thought come from? Chelsea is my best friend. Why am I thinking such mean things about my best friend?

"I must ask you to keep quiet until I'm through," Chelsea says.

What!

"Well, you'd better be through soon," Bri says, standing, hands on her hips. "I'm about to slap you upside the head."

"Soon, we will be going into the seventh grade," Chelsea continues. "Then high school. We must be prepared. We must have a plan."

"A plan for what?" Nicole asks.

"A plan to make sure we're still popular in high school!" Chelsea slaps her desk for emphasis.

She's lost her mind. She's absolutely lost her mind. A club so we can be popular. Bri is doubled over, she's laughing so hard.

Nicole, on the other hand, is very serious. "Are we popular now?" she asks, turning to me, wondering if she's been popular this whole time and didn't know it.

Which makes me laugh. The idea of Nicole being popular. The idea of forming a club just to be popular.

"Are you with me?" Chelsea asks. "I need to know if you are with me."

With her?

"What's the name of this club?" Bri asks.

"Well, that's something we need to vote on," Chelsea says.

"How about 'the Popular Girls'?" Nicole offers. Like I said, 40 watts.

Bri snickers.

"A little obvious, Nick," Chelsea says.

"How about 'the Soul Sisters'?" Bri asks.

We shake our heads.

"How about 'Keila's Crew'?" Keila says, laughing. "Kidding."

Kei hasn't said much about Josh since the slumber party when we mailed him the letter. I ask Kei if she's heard from him yet, and she says no. But he's been looking at her in study hall!

"How about 'the Hot Chicks'!" Bri yells, joking around.

"'The Dixie Chicks'!" Nicole yells.

"That's a band," Keila says.

"I like the way it sounds," Nicole says.

"'The Wild Women'!" Kei says.

Chelsea shakes her head. "Something meaningful," she says.

"I know! I know!" Bri says.

"What? What?" we all shout.

"'Five Pretty Girls Who Need to Be Kissed'! That's meaningful!"

"Ugh!" We all roll around on the floor, arms wrapped around our stomachs.

"I've got it! I've got it!" I yell.

"What?" everyone yells.

"'The Mona Lisas'!" I say. "Like the song, 'Mona Lisas and Mad Hatters.' Elton John. . . ."

No one says anything. I guess my mom's the only one who plays Elton John.

Then Chelsea says, "I like it."

"Me, too," Nicole says, as if it's okay to admit it now that Chelsea has said she likes it.

"The Mona Lisas," Chelsea whispers.

"All in favor of the 'Mona Lisas,' raise your hand," Chelsea says.

Five hands shoot up. Our first unanimous vote, and it's for the name I picked. I'm feeling a little better now.

"All in favor of meeting here every Wednesday after school say 'aye,'" Chelsea says.

"Aye," we all say.

"Okay," Chelsea says. "Now let's talk about uniforms. I was thinking we should—"

Bri leaps to her feet. "Uniforms! Uniforms! Are you kidding?" Her hands are on her hips. You don't want to mess with Bri when her hands are on her hips.

"Well, not exactly uniforms," Chelsea says. "But we need to stand out from everyone else."

"Out or above?" Bri says. *Ouch!*

"I was thinking we should all wear pink tops on Fridays," Chelsea says.

Bri jumps up again. "Pink! Pink! This girl does not

wear pink!" She's pointing to herself and wiggling her head back and forth. She's so funny.

"Well, it doesn't have to be pink. . . ."

"Yellow?" Nicole offers.

Keila stands up and imitates Bri. "This girl does not wear yellow."

"Purple?" Bri says. Everyone is quiet for a minute.

"Lime green?" offers Nicole. Bri and I roll our eyeballs at each other. Like everyone has a lime green shirt. Like *anyone* looks good in lime green.

"Red," Keila says. "The Mona Lisas should wear red shirts or sweaters and black pants."

Hmmm.

"All in favor of red shirts and black pants say 'aye,'" Kei says.

"Hey! I'm supposed to say that!" Chelsea says. "All in favor of red shirts and black pants say 'aye.'"

"Aye!" we all say. Except Bri.

"And what color undies would you like me to wear?" she asks.

Chelsea glares at her.

"I have an idea!" Nicole shouts.

"Better than uniforms?" Bri asks.

"Let's have a special thing we say at the end of each meeting."

"Like what?" Chelsea asks.

"How about 'TTFN'!" Nicole says.

"TTFN?"

"Ta-ta for now!"

Bri and I just look at each other, like *puhlease*. But before we get to say a word, Chelsea jumps on it like a boy giving you a flat on the back of your shoe.

"I like it," she says.

Then Mrs. Gardner sticks her head in and says it's time for dinner.

"Ta-ta for now!" Nicole says. No one follows her lead.

I wait for everyone to leave. I need to talk to Chelsea alone.

"Wasn't the first meeting of the Mona Lisas great, Lyss?" Chelsea asks.

"Yeah, great," I say. "I—"

"I can't wait until the next meeting," Chelsea says, pirouetting around the room like she's in ballet class.

"Chels, I have to tell you about something that happened this weekend!" I say, exasperated. She's not paying attention to me at all!

"We'll be the most popular girls in school. And I'll be president!" she says, dancing in her own little world. She's starting to freak me out. "Do you think we should invite Hayden? She's been calling me a lot lately. She really wants to be friends. I feel kind of sorry for her."

"No way! If you do I'll—"

"Or is six people too many?" she asks, still dancing around the room.

"Too many. Chels, I—"

But she's lost in her own little world. I sigh and walk out the door, wondering if she will even notice I'm gone. What has happened to my best friend? When did she become such an egomaniac?

"Good night, Mrs. Gardner."

"Good night, Alyssa. Would you like to stay for supper?"

Mrs. Gardner is the best. She's the way a mom should be. Old-fashioned. For some reason, just looking at her makes me want to cry.

I can smell meatloaf and potatoes or something all-American and hearty cooking in Mrs. G.'s kitchen. Something normal. It smells so good. I think about the health food waiting for me at home.

"I'd love to," I say, and it's the truth. "But I really need to get home."

"Well, actually, your mom called and she's going to be a little late getting home from work, so if you want to stay—" Mrs. G. puts an arm around my shoulders. She really cares about me, which is more than I can say for her daughter.

"I'm okay," I say, lying. I'm not okay, but I can't stay here. I feel like I'm going to cry. Being here makes me feel even worse. I rush out the front door.

I walk slowly down Court Street. The sun is warm on my face, and a cool breeze blows through the trees. I pass the corner store where I usually get candy. I walk and walk.

I sing the Mona Lisa song quietly, kick a stone, kick it again when I catch up to it. It just misses a little sparrow pecking at something on the sidewalk.

Kick, kick, kick.

The pebble hits the black gate of St. Mary's Star of the Sea Church. I look up at the steeple, the huge steps, the stained glass.

I have always felt peaceful and safe here. I open the gate and walk through.

As I climb the steps, the weirdest thing happens. A song I haven't thought of in a long time pops into my head. My mom used to sing it to me when I was little, before I went to sleep. I called it "The Tuck-in Song." As I open the heavy wooden doors of the church, I hear the song about God's eye being on the sparrow and watching over me.

And my mother saying *"Sogni d'oro."* Sweet dreams.

9

sparrows

Someone call the *New York Post*: Alyssa Fontana is actually going to church, and no one is making her!

I can't believe I'm walking into church. I *never* want to go to church. And it isn't even Sunday!

Being Italian, I've always heard about God, mainly Jesus. You can't turn a corner in Nonna's house without running into Jesus or Mary. But my mom isn't into God like Nonna and my aunts are. So I've always wondered if Jesus is like, O.F. Old-fashioned.

My friend Sarah is Jewish, and she believes some of the same things Catholics believe, like Noah's Ark and the Ten Commandments, but she doesn't believe the Jesus part. And some people think Jesus was a teacher, but not God, and that Allah is the real God. Some people (women, mainly) say that God is a woman, and others say that they are all the same God with different names, which really confuses me.

And then there are those nice people who knock on our apartment door with the perfect suits and dresses, nice smiles, and little booklets. They're *really* into God and seem to know a lot about the whole thing, but everyone laughs at them. When Bri sees them coming, she doesn't even answer the door.

It used to be that people only mentioned God when you sneezed, but ever since September 11, when the World Trade Center was attacked, you hear people talking about God all the time. Every time you turn around, someone is saying "God bless America."

The last rays of the day's light stream in through the stained glass windows. Dust dances in the bright beams that touch a pew here, a pew there. Candles burn, and I smell incense.

I walk back to the little bowl with the holy water (I forgot to stick my fingers in it when I came in), make the sign of the cross, then walk slowly down the left aisle, running my hand along the smooth wood. I sit down in a ray of sunlight at the end of a pew and stare up at Jesus on the cross.

Sometimes I wish I lived back when Jesus did, so I could see him walking on the earth, laughing with people, healing people. But then I remember. They didn't have Trixie Belden books or TVs or ballet or ice cream sandwiches back then. And they lived in the desert and had to wear long robes with no deodorant.

So I guess it's not that I really want to live back when

Jesus did. I just want to know that people didn't make the whole Jesus thing up to make themselves feel better, and there's really no one out there to protect me after all.

I feel guilty for thinking like that, but it's true, and I bet a lot of other people feel that way, too, if they would only admit it. Some people act like they have just had Jesus over for dinner, like he's just passed the potatoes to them personally or something. Like they are so close. Not me. I've always thought he was floating above the clouds somewhere.

And then there's the Virgin Mary. Italians love the Virgin Mary, Catholics love the Virgin Mary, and I don't feel a thing when I look at her.

There must be something wrong with me. I better try harder.

I sit down on a pew about five rows back, not so close that I'm in God's face, not so far that he won't notice me. I kneel down on the little padded bench thing.

Now what? *Our Father?* Ten *Hail Marys?* The only other prayer I can think of is "Now I Lay Me Down to Sleep."

And so I say, "Our Father, who art in Heaven. Hallowed be thy name." And stop. It sounds so weird.

Who says *hallowed* these days anyway? And what exactly does it mean? I feel guilty for questioning such a thing.

I start to leave, but something pulls me back.

So I wait.

Nothing happens.

I wait some more.

Nothing happens.

Argh!

Well, maybe I should just talk to him the way I do to my friends. Maybe he won't mind.

"Uh, God? It's me, Alyssa Fontana. You probably know my grandmother? Maria Feraco? She seems to know you pretty good."

I look at the ceiling, the beautiful wood beams. "I've been pretty upset lately. I don't even know if I like my best friend anymore. She doesn't seem to care about anyone but herself. And I just found out that my dad left us. *He didn't die.* He just left us, which is much worse than if he had died. If he had died, he might have still loved us. But he left, so he must not have loved us. And that really hurts," I say, crying.

And then I get angry. Really angry. "How could you let him leave us? Why didn't you stop him?" I say to the ceiling.

And then I think about that. What could God have

done? Reached down from heaven with a giant hand, plucked Dad and his suitcases out of the car, and plopped him back in our apartment? But still . . . it seems like he should have done something!

"And I'm kind of scared, too. The whole World Trade Center thing. Where were you when that happened? Nothing feels safe anymore. It's just not right!" My voice cracks. I start crying again.

"Can you hear me? Are you listening? Are you there? Do you care? I really need someone right now. . . ." *I really need you to be real.*

And then I notice a discarded missalette on the pew next to me. I flip it open to a reading from the Gospel of St. Luke:

> Are not five sparrows sold for two copper
> coins? And not one of them is forgotten
> before God. But the very hairs of your head
> are all numbered. Do not fear therefore; you
> are of more value than many sparrows.

The sparrow. Huh. Like "The Tuck-in Song," the song about the sparrow that was playing in my head as I walked into church. Weird.

The song starts playing again, the words filling me up inside, making me feel safe.

10

PEPPERONI

Something is sticking out of the top shelf of my locker. Popsicle sticks. Sticky orange Popsicle sticks stuck through the air vents.

Hayden got me again. The worst part is that she never does anything to me when anyone is looking, so no one believes me when I say how mean she is.

I look down the hall toward her locker. She's talking to Nicole. Before you know it, she'll be in the Mona Lisas, and I won't have any friends at all. Then what will I do?

"Hey, Lyss," Dillon says, as I close the door to my locker with a bang.

"Hey," I say, walking toward room 203 for English class.

"How's it hangin'?" he asks, laughing.

"What?"

He reaches behind me and snaps my bra, then runs down the hall laughing. I get it now, the jerk.

"Hey, Dillon! You are *so* history!" I yell after him. But he's already around the corner and doesn't hear me. I walk into English class and sit down in my assigned-in-alphabetical-order seat next to Anthony Focaccia and Elizabeth Forest-Harding.

"What's up, Cheese?" Anthony says. Anthony likes to confuse my last name, Fontana, with Fontina, which is a cheese. Pretty nervy for a guy named after a messy bread.

"What's up with you, Breadman?"

This is a daily ritual.

Mr. Carter hands out last week's assignment. Mr. Carter is the youngest and cutest teacher in the whole school. I wish I could flunk English just so I could see him every day for the rest of my life. He has short brown hair and one of those beards that connects to his mustache. His smile is huge, bright white, and his eyes dance when he talks, like he always thinks we are funny. Which is an improvement over Ms. Randall, who definitely did not think we were funny at all.

Last week's assignment was to write about our families. We were supposed to find something in particular to write about, a theme, not just list our relatives. It was really hard to come up with a theme.

But I thought and thought and thought, and then I

remembered some stories my family told me years ago. Most of the stories centered around food and romance, as if one leads to the other (which it might, in my family!).

Nonna met my grandfather, Carmen Feraco, during the Feast of San Gennaro in Little Italy. Nonna had never seen so many people or so much food in her life. People were dancing in the streets, and she joined them, her bright red-yellow-and-green dress twirling around and around. Nonna was thin and beautiful back then, or so she says, and Nonno Carmen could not take his eyes off her. (Or so she claims.)

Nonno grabbed Nonna's hand, and they ran together to the table where Carmen's friend was selling food for the festival, where they shared the first of many pepperoni sandwiches.

I wrote about my mother, the youngest of the Feraco women. When my mother was young, she used to work for Uncle Louie's butcher. She helped make the sausage and pepperoni. First she put the meat through a grinder, then added curing salt, seasoning, and citric acid (to make it tart). Then she used a stuffer to stuff the casings. Then she smoked it. She did this over and over, and now she's a vegetarian.

Aunt Louisa met Uncle Chito at Figaro's on her lunch

break from Wanamaker's Department Store. She ordered an antipasto with extra pepperoni, peppers, and anchovies. Chito listened carefully, ordered the same thing, then came up beside her and said, "Can you believe we just ordered the same thing?" He asked her to have lunch with him, and she did. Louisa later learned that Chito does indeed love peppers and pepperoni—but hates anchovies . . . but he thought she was the prettiest thing he'd ever seen and was willing to eat anything just to meet her. (So romantic!)

When Aunt Elena met Uncle Louie, Uncle Louie didn't have the big restaurant he has now in Little Italy. He had a small take-out place in Brooklyn Heights near Elena's hair salon. When Uncle Louie showed up one day to have his hair cut instead of going to Dom the barber, Elena knew he was interested in her. She stopped by his pizzeria the next day with homemade pepperoni breadsticks, and it's been love ever since. (Aunt Elena says that the secret to good breadsticks is that you must beat the dough with exactly twenty strokes. She told me not to tell anyone, but she uses baking mix from the store.)

I don't think Uncle Dom has ever had a significant pepperoni experience.

"Alyssa, this is the funniest paper I've ever read," Mr. Carter says.

An A+. Cool. In the margins it says "funny," "cute," and "I'd love to meet your family!"

He hands Breadman his paper. A C+. I would die if I got a C.

"Nice job," Mr. Carter whispers to Weezer Hayes, who sits behind me. Weezer is one of the smartest kids in our class. We call him Weezer because he has asthma and sometimes he makes this loud noise when he breathes. It's kind of mean, but he doesn't seem to mind. I can't even remember his real name. Mostly, he keeps to himself. He doesn't seem to have that many friends. Could be because he's not too good-looking, and his clothes look old and tired.

Mr. Carter is not happy with the rest of the class papers.

"What, do you people live in caves? Except for one or two of you, you do not have even the most basic comprehension of punctuation or grammar. If your lives depended on the proper use of a comma, you'd all be dead."

"There were only a handful of good papers, and only one outstanding one, which I'm going to hand out to you as an example."

Everyone starts whispering, trying to figure out who wrote the good paper. Someone says Elizabeth Forest-Harding, I guess because she has a hyphen in her name, so she must know about other punctuation marks. I hear Weezer's name mentioned. I don't hear my name mentioned even once, which kind of annoys me, but when Mr. Carter passes out the "outstanding" paper as an example for the rest of the class, it's "Pepperoni: A Love Story," written by yours truly.

I feel eyes boring into my back and turn around to see Hayden staring at me.

Mr. Carter asks me to read my paper out loud while the class follows along. This would not have been so bad if he hadn't kept interrupting me to show how I'd used the comma before the conjunction in the compound sentence and so on. I thought I'd never get through it. And every time I said "pepperoni," Breadman laughed hysterically. Who knows what that's about.

I know about commas and stuff because I read all the time. I study everything. I study when a comma is used and when it isn't. I look up any words I don't know and write the definition in a notebook.

When we're leaving class that day, Breadman says, "Way to go, Cheese. Can I have some pepperoni with that, Cheese?" He thinks he's so funny.

"For your focaccia, Breadman?" That shuts him up.

Hayden isn't nearly as easy to deal with. I find pepperoni slices on the top shelf of my locker for weeks.

11

THE VOTE

Our next assignment for English class is to start keeping a journal. We are supposed to write in it every day for the rest of the year. We can pretend we're writing to a friend if we have trouble getting started.

Mr. Carter says we can write about anything at all and he won't read it. Everyone went nuts when he said that! If he isn't going to read it, what is the point of writing it? He says that he just wants to get us writing, that we can write what is most important to us, even personal stuff. He will ask us to bring it in every once in a while to see that we are writing, but not to see *what* we are writing. He wants us to learn to love writing. I think the idea is pretty cool, myself.

Mr. Carter suggests a few topics, in case we had no ideas. He says we can write about what we want to be when we grow up, who we respect the most, our favorite food, our favorite holiday and why, our favorite book and why, our favorite movie and why.

Chelsea's teacher assigned the same thing! Chelsea says she's going to keep a running list of the boys that she likes and why, and rank them. I told her that I don't think that's what they have in mind.

A list of boys! I'm beginning to think that Chelsea is just a little bit shallow.

After the next meeting of the Mona Lisas, I'm definitely thinking she's shallow. It's the meeting where we vote for officers. Chelsea says we need a president, a secretary, and a treasurer.

"Who wants to be president?" Bri yells.

"I'm going to be president," Chelsea says, standing.

"But I thought we are supposed to vote," Keila says.

"Yes. Let's start with the secretary," Chelsea says, sitting down. "The secretary will keep the notes of the meeting. You know, write down what we talk about."

Duh. Like we don't know what a secretary is. Bri and I roll our eyeballs at each other.

Chelsea hands out little pieces of paper with "TML" at the top. "Write down the name of the person you think should be secretary on the piece of paper, fold it, and then put it in front of me on my desk."

I look down at my little blank piece of paper. Who should be secretary? I look over at Bri's paper out of the corner of my eye. She pulls it to her chest like it's some major secret or something. I look at Nicole, who is writing my name down on the tiny slip of paper.

Me! I don't want to be secretary! So I write down Bri's name and hand it to Chelsea.

Chelsea opens the first one. "Alyssa," she says, starting a pile for my votes.

She opens the second. "Alyssa," she says. She opens each one with great care, like it's the Academy Awards or something.

The third: "Alyssa." *Great.*

Then, "Oh, here's one for Bri!"

And finally, "Well, Alyssa, it looks like you are our new secretary!"

Everyone claps. I try to look enthusiastic about my new position.

"Anything you want to say, Alyssa?" Chelsea asks.

Puhlease. I glare at her.

"Okay, then," Chelsea says, handing us more white slips of paper. "Now for the treasurer position."

"What's a treasurer?" Nicole asks.

"Didn't you ever go to Brownies?" Bri says. *Duh!*

"No," Nicole says, blushing.

"The treasurer will keep track of all the money, like dues, that kind of thing," Chelsea says.

With no hesitation, I write "Keila" on mine, fold it

up, and hand it back to Chelsea. Keila is, by far, the best at math of all of us, which, now that I think about it, is kind of weird for a funky artistic chick.

The vote is unanimous. Keila it is.

"Speaking of Keila, next Wednesday is the big day," Bri says. "Keila and Josh sitting in a tree. K-I-S-S-I-N-G."

"You are so immature!" Keila says.

That night I write in my journal. (I named my journal Gabbie. "Dear Journal" seems too stupid to me.)

> Dear Gabbie,
> Today the Mona Lisas voted me in as Secretary. I guess because I'm the best writer.
> I'm still not sure how I feel about this Mona Lisas thing. Chelsea is acting so weird. I wish we could go back to 5th grade, when things weren't so confusing.
> Keila finds out about Josh next week! We've all been dying to know if he likes her. Will he wear the yellow-and-blue shirt?
> Mr. Carter is really cute. When he smiles, my heart flips and my stomach jumps and I usually say something stupid. Is that love?

12

LOVE NOTE

Something is sticking out of the top of my locker *again*.
At least this time it isn't a gooey Popsicle stick or a slice
of pepperoni. It looks like a piece of paper.

I open my locker and grab it, looking up and down
the hallway to see if anyone is watching.

Someone has cut letters out of a magazine and past-
ed them on the page. Creepy. It says:

**I LOVE YOU, ALYSSA
MEET ME AT THE PICNIC TABLE
AFTER SCHOOL TOMORROW
IT'S TIME WE TALK**

I look up and down the hall, both ways, to see if
anyone, like the writer of the note, is watching me. No
one is looking. I fold it up and stick it in my notebook.

It's kind of creepy because of the cut-out letters, but
also exciting. I need to talk to Chelsea right away!

In social studies, I hand her the note. Her eyes widen. Chelsea *lives* for this stuff.

She hands it back and whispers, "What will you wear?"

What will I wear? It wasn't exactly my first thought! Like, first of all, who wrote it? Who's in love with me?

I shrug and rip a piece of notepaper out of my notebook. (Ooh. So loud!) I look over my shoulder to see what Ms. Simon is doing. She's still handing out last week's homework assignment.

"I don't know. Who do you think it is?" I write, passing the paper to Chelsea.

"Wear your red sweater and black jeans. I don't know," she writes, handing the note back to me.

"You think I should go?" I write and pass the note to her.

She looks at me like, *duh!*

"Will you come with me?" I write quickly.

"Absolutely," she writes.

That night, I can't sleep. All I can think about is my mystery man.

I look at the alarm clock. Ten p.m. I grab my journal.

Dear Gabbie,
    A boy left a love note in my locker
today. I can't believe it! I wonder who it's

from. Maybe Jason Andrews, wouldn't
that be great? He's so cute. Or maybe . . .
Mr. Carter? Maybe that's why we have to
meet in secret, because he's my teacher
and dating him isn't allowed!

I love Mr. Carter. He makes me feel
happy and safe.

Sometimes I get a bad feeling about the
note, though. Why did the person use cut-out
letters instead of writing the note by
hand? Kind of creepy.

It would be great to have a boyfriend.
A real boyfriend. Someone to hold hands
with. Someone to buy presents for on
Valentine's Day and Christmas. Dillon
doesn't do any of that stuff. He's so
immature.

Maybe I could become part of Mr.
Carter's family. We'd all have dinner and
we'd eat normal food and watch TV
together. Maybe Keila and Josh and me
and Mr. Carter can double-date! Wouldn't
that be great? We'll go out to dinner as
couples!

Maybe it is Mr. Carter!!!! Did I tell you

that he smells really good? He definitely likes me, but maybe it's only because I'm a good writer.

I forgot. He's going to look at this one of these days! I'd better cross his name out. But I've written it in so many places.

I'm so tired right now. I'll do it tomorrow.

Good night, Gabs.

13

THE MYSTERY MAN

Beeeeep, beeeeep, beeeeep, beeeeep!

We're being invaded by aliens! Invaded by aliens!

I sit straight up in my bed, my heart pounding. It's the buzzer on the clock radio. Usually I set the alarm to "Radio," so music will play, but I must have set it to "Buzzer" by mistake. Argh! I fall back onto my pillow.

I'm so tired! That's what I get for staying up all night writing in my journal.

I hit the snooze button.

Beeeeep, beeeeep, beeeeep, beeeeep!

Snooze.

Beeeeep, beeeeep, beeeeep, beeeeep!

"Alyssa! Alyssa! Are you up, honey?" Mom yells.

Oh, no! I'm *so* late, and today is my big day!

I run into the bathroom, almost running over Mom on the way. I turn on the water in the shower. *C'mon, warm up.* There is never any hot water in Brooklyn at this hour of the morning. Argh! That's what I get for getting up late. But I have to wash my hair. I have to! I jump into the cold blast.

Strawberry Essence? Peach Divine? Just grab one, it's cold and it's late!

I shampoo my hair, wash fast. As water trickles down the front of me, I note once again that my chest is *still flat*.

I run to my room, almost slipping in the puddles I leave on the hardwood floor. I blow-dry my hair upside down for more body, a trick Chelsea taught me. It looks pretty good! I spray myself head to toe with Passion's Promise body mist.

I put on the red sweater that Chelsea said I should wear. My mom gave it to me for Valentine's Day. I was so embarrassed when she gave it to me. Valentine's Day is not a day for moms. It's for boyfriends. But I'm glad she gave it to me now. It looks great, especially with my new black jeans and boots. I put in some dangly earrings, just as Mom yells, "Alyssa! Are you ready yet?"

"You look nice," she says when I come out of my room.

"Thanks."

"No time for breakfast, so I put some trail mix in a bag for you."

I thank her and take the bag. It's the thought that counts.

I barely make it to school on time. During study hall, I write in my journal.

Dear Gabs,
Today is the slowest day. Every time I look at the clock, it hasn't moved! I can't wait until school is over.

Then I draw hearts. Plain hearts. Hearts with flowers around them. Hearts with arrows through them. Meanwhile, the clock ticks by so slowly I wonder if it's broken. Finally, just when I think the day will never end, the bell rings.

I run to my locker to meet Chelsea. She's late. I look at my watch. I'm supposed to be at the picnic table right after school, and the bell rang ten minutes ago. I'll wait two more minutes.

I look up the hall. No Chelsea. I look down the hall. No Chelsea. I can't believe she isn't here.

Boys are playing basketball, and some girls are flirting with the boys playing basketball. No one is at the picnic table. I can't believe it.

I walk over, sit down, look around. I run a hand through my hair. I check my earrings. Fine. I check my armpits. Deodorant still working. I smell my wrists. Passion's Promise is faint, but still there. I put on some lip-gloss and run my finger along my lips to make sure it doesn't lump up. Perfect. But where is my mystery man?

Finally, out of the corner of my eye, I notice someone coming around the corner of the school. My heart jumps.

Then falls into the pit of my stomach. It's Weezer.

I feel like I'm going to cry. No way!

"Hi, Alyssa," he says shyly. He sees my face and looks confused.

"I got this note," he says, showing me a note identical to mine. Behind me, I hear people laughing and whistling.

I nod, trying not to cry, trying not to make Weezer feel bad. I hold up my note. "Someone's playing a trick on us." My voice shakes.

"I should have figured," Weezer says, looking over his shoulder.

I follow his eyes. Dillon, Zack, Bri, Nicole, Hayden, and some older girls I don't know are all staring at us. Staring at me and Weezer. And laughing. Well, some of them. The rest look confused.

"I've gotta go," I grab my backpack. "I'm sorry, Weez." I walk away, fast.

"David," he calls after me. "My name is David."

"David," I say, as I back away. I don't want to hurt his feelings. But I have to go.

There is a lump in my throat. A block from school, I burst into tears.

So much for my mystery man.

14

THE MEANEST TRICK

Dear Gabbie,

The mystery man turned out to be Weezer! Well, sort of. He didn't write the note. I couldn't believe it. I thought I would burst into tears right there, but I managed not to freak. I didn't want to make Weezer feel bad. I could tell he felt pretty bad, too. I bet he wants a girlfriend, just like I want a boyfriend.

This was so mean. So mean. She really went too far this time. She embarrassed me in front of everyone. She embarrassed Weezer in front of everyone.

I'm going to get her. I swear, I'm going to get her. I wish Hayden Martin had never come to our school. Things were so much better before she came.

And Chelsea never showed up. Some friend!

Maybe she was in on it. Maybe she's buddies with Hayden now.

Okay, now I'm losing it. Chelsea may be shallow, but she's not mean.

I don't even want to go to the Mona Lisas meeting tomorrow. But I have to. I have to talk to Chelsea and Nicole and Bri. Why wasn't Chelsea there? Why were Bri and Nicole there and what do they know?

I'm going to find out. And someone is going to pay.

15

THE PERFECT WORDS

"What's up, Cheese?" Breadman says when I walk into English class.

"Shut up, Breadman." I scan the room for Weezer, I mean, David, and Hayden. Weezer is staring at a notebook and not meeting my eyes. Hayden is looking at me and whispering to Karla Mooney. And laughing. Is she laughing about me and Weezer and how she humiliated us?

"Did you study for the spelling test?" Elizabeth F-H whispers as I sit down.

Spelling test? Argh!

I hate these tests! If Mr. Carter asked me how to spell something, I could tell him. But when he gives us four different choices to choose from, they all start to look good, and I'm completely confused.

"You have fifteen minutes to complete the test," Mr. Carter says.

We all groan.

"Oh, stop your whining. You've known about this for a week."

"I totally forgot about it," I whisper to Elizabeth F-H. I had other things on my mind.

"Please pass me your journals. I'll take a look at them while you're taking the test."

I stare down at the words on the page. "Embarrass" is the hardest one. I can never remember whether there are two *R*'s or two *S*'s or both.

I whiz through the spelling test and decide to put the words in sentences for extra credit. If you put the words in sentences, spell them correctly, and the sentences make sense and are related, like they are actually about something, you get a homework pass, which means you can skip the homework assignment of your choice.

So far, no one has been able to pull it off. And today's words are really hard.

I write:

This miscreant, whose name I won't mention but has frizzy hair and is the meanest girl in school, exhibited aberrant behavior by setting me up for a clandestine meeting with a supposed admirer. But it

was just a mean trick. I am <u>incensed</u> and
want to yell <u>epithets</u> at the person who is
responsible, whose name I won't mention
but is sitting in the back row and has
frizzy hair and is the meanest girl in
school, because I have been <u>maligned</u> and
am now totally <u>embarrassed</u>. Plus, my best
friend was supposed to be there, but she
wasn't, which is an <u>enigma</u> to me.
<u>Practically</u>, I should just get over it, but
lately she seems to be friendship deficient,
and I'm pretty upset about it.

Wow, the perfect words this week! It's just like Mr.
Carter had been reading my journal when he picked
them out.

My journal! Oh, no, my journal! I forgot to cross Mr.
Carter's name out in my journal!

I look at him out of the corner of my eye. I wonder
where my journal is in the pile. I wonder if I should try
to get it back from him.

It looks like he's just flipping through them to see
how much we've written, not *what* we've written, just like
he said he would do. But how can he miss his name in
my journal when there are all those hearts around it?

I feel my face turning red as I sink down in my chair.

I study his face for a sign as he collects our tests and hands back our journals. But there is none. I'm never going to know whether he knows I'm in love with him.

I'm going to cry. I'm going to die.

And then I see it. Written on an empty desk in front of me: "Alyssa & Weezer." In a heart.

I scribble it out, and as Elizabeth F-H reads her book report to the class, I draw a butterfly so I can fly, fly away.

16

Drama Queens

I'm late getting to the next meeting of the Mona Lisas. Between the Weezer situation and the Mr. Carter situation, I'm really down. Poor Weezer, wanting a girlfriend and it turns out to be me, and I don't like him. Well, not that way, anyway. Poor me, hoping for Mr. Right and it turns out to be Mr. Wrong. Poor me again—Mr. Carter might know I'm in love with him! And I don't even know if he knows! I don't even know whether to be totally humiliated or not.

And I'm still upset about my dad, alive and well and living in the suburbs of southern California. I'd like to pluck out his eyeballs for leaving my mom and me. For being so selfish.

Let's see if he can surf with no eyeballs. If he surfs. I don't even know. And I don't care.

He must have a girlfriend. I'm afraid to ask my mom.

If God is real, why are all these bad things happening

to me? Yo! Up there! You're supposed to be looking out for me! Ya know, your little sparrow?

Mrs. Gardner is ironing and watching *Oprah* when I walk in the door. I rush down the hall to Chelsea's room.

She's sitting at her desk staring at a notebook. I wonder if we're in for a speech. When I walk into the room, she says, "Well, now that Alyssa is here, I guess we can start. Alyssa, can you read the minutes of the last meeting?"

Minutes? I stare at her blankly. Was I supposed to write something down? Oops.

"Ah . . . um . . . well . . ." I grab my backpack and pull out my journal, tilting it up so no one can see. "Yes, well, we voted in officers. Chelsea is president, I am secretary, and Keila is treasurer."

"And was everyone present?" Chelsea asks, staring out her bedroom window, twirling a strand of hair around her finger.

"Yes, everyone was present."

"Okay. Does anyone have any agenda items for today?"

"Keila!" everyone yells.

Keila blushes. "He wore the shirt!"

"*Yes!*" We slap each other five.

"I can't believe it!"

"I want a Double Dare!" someone shouts.

"Are you going out?" Bri asks.

"I think so," Kei says.

Whoa! I can't believe it!

When everyone calms down, I raise my hand.

"Alyssa, you are recognized," Chelsea says. *Recognized?* Where does she get this stuff?

"C-SPAN," Bri whispers, giggling.

"I want to know who knows anything—and I mean anything—about Weezer and the love note."

"Huh?" Bri says, confused, having never heard Weezer's name and the word "love" in the same sentence.

"Someone left a love note in my locker and said to meet him after school. And when I got there, it was Weezer!"

Chelsea and Bri fall over laughing, holding their stomachs.

"It's not funny!"

"Weezer's in love with you?" Bri says, rolling on the floor.

"No, he's not, I mean, well, I don't know if he is. He didn't send the note. It was a trick, a mean trick."

"And why weren't you there?" I yell, standing up

and pointing at Chelsea. "You were supposed to come with me."

Everyone looks at Chelsea, who says, nodding, "Okay, put it on the agenda."

Agenda? "No! I want to talk about it now!" I shout, throwing my pretend meeting minutes at her, praying no one opens up my journal to see what's inside.

"This meeting will come to order!" Chelsea says, slapping her brush on her desk. "God, Alyssa, you are such a *drama queen*!"

That's it! "You are . . . You are such a . . . (I want to say "drama queen" but Chelsea already did) . . . *prima donna*!" I use one of Nonna's words on her.

"What's a prima donna?" Nicole whispers.

"Must mean she thinks the whole world revolves around her," Bri says.

Back to the subject. "Does anyone know who did this?" I hold up the note, not wanting to say Hayden's name, because they never believe me when I tell them she's picking on me. I want to hear them say it. *Say it!*

"Probably Dillon," Bri says. "Didn't you just dump him?"

What? Dillon? No way. "I never *officially* dumped him."

"Well, if he thinks you broke up with him, maybe he's getting back at you," Keila says.

Nicole nods. Like she knows anything.

"You know who did this," I say, pointing at Bri. "I saw you with her! I saw you with her that day!" Tears are rolling down my cheeks now.

"Who?" Bri says, confused.

"Hayden. Who else? The girl who has been picking on me since she came here." I wipe a hand across my face.

No one says a word.

Finally, Keila says, "I don't think it's Hayden. I don't think she's *that* mean."

"She put gum in my hair!" I yell.

"Maybe it was an accident," Chelsea says.

I cannot believe it. I can*not* believe it. They are defending Hayden!

"What's wrong with you guys? What's wrong with you? Whose side are you on?" Everyone is staring at me. I don't care.

"This whole club is stupid!" I shout. "At least the Bob-Whites *did* something. At least they solved mysteries!"

"Who are the Bob-Whites?" Nicole whispers to Bri.

"Trixie Belden and the Bob-Whites. A bunch of friends who helped other people and did cool things, which is more than I can say for this stupid club!"

I'm pacing back and forth. "This stupid club is all about Chelsea!" I say, pointing.

Everyone turns and stares at Chelsea, the Prima Donna President.

"Wh-wh-what?" Chelsea stammers.

"Everyone who thinks Chelsea is a prima donna, say 'aye'!"

"Does that mean she's bossy and thinks too much of herself?" Nicole asks.

"Yes," I say.

"Aye!" everyone says.

Chelsea's face goes white. She looks like she's going to pass out.

"Everyone who thinks this club is stupid say 'aye'!"

"Aye!" everyone says.

"Everyone who thinks this meeting is over say 'aye'!" I'm starting to feel powerful.

"Aye!" everyone says, standing.

"Ta-ta for now." Nicole waves good-bye to Chelsea.

We walk out of Chelsea's room with Chelsea staring after us, quiet for once.

Bri and I walk together for a few blocks.

"I kind of liked the idea of the club," Bri says.

"No way."

"No, really."

"I thought you would think you were too cool for it."

"Well, I am," Bri laughs. "You are, too."

We walk in silence until we get to her corner.

"Hey, Bri. Find out who sent that note!"

"I'll try!" She disappears into the night.

I walk slowly up Court Street, kicking a stone, the wind blowing back my hair. It's a nice night, but all I see is dark. I feel guilty for being mean to Chelsea. Why are people so messed up?

Best friends should listen to you when you talk and not act like dictators.

People shouldn't stick love notes in lockers and get your hopes up and hurt people.

Girls shouldn't put gum in your hair.

The boys you want to love you should, and the ones you don't want to love you shouldn't.

I kick at a pebble, just missing a little brown bird on the sidewalk.

Teachers should *not* know you have crushes on them.

Mothers should not be vegetarians.

Fathers shouldn't leave.

And as I walk by St. Mary's Star of the Sea Church I think, *and God should talk to you out loud.*

The bird stops, cocks its head, and looks up.

17

MEATLOAF

Mom hands me the phone as I walk in the door.

As soon as I say "Hello," I'm hit by a rush of words.

"Alyssa! How could you? How could you?" she starts.

Then, "We've been friends for a long time, Alyssa."

Then, "What's wrong with you?"

That's it. "What's wrong with *me*? What's wrong with *me*? Are you kidding? What's wrong with *you*? When did you decide to become president of the world?"

She hangs up.

"Everything okay, Alyssa? Was that Chelsea?" Mom asks.

"Why can't you make meatloaf like everyone else!" I yell and run into my room. I jump into bed and bury my head under the pillow.

"What?" she asks, standing next to my bed, sounding confused.

"Why can't you make meatloaf and potatoes like

everyone else? And why did you give me four first names? Why can't we be normal like everyone else?" I start crying.

"No one is 'normal,' Alyssa. You'll find that out when you get older." Mom sits down next to me, runs a hand through my hair. "What's going on?"

I sit up, arms across my chest, tears running down my face. "I just want meatloaf. Why can't you make meatloaf!"

Mom plays along, even though I sound like a four-year-old. "I have a great recipe for vegetarian meatloaf," she says.

"No! Not vegetarian—with hamburger, like everyone else!"

"Okay, I can do that," Mom says. "That will be a lot of hamburger for one girl." She strokes my head. It feels so good. "Now, do you want to tell me what's really going on?"

"Hayden sent me a love note and Chelsea is a dictator and people are getting shot on TV and the World Trade Center attack and Dillon snapped my bra and I'm still flat as a board and you cook weird food and Mr. Carter knows I love him and Daddy doesn't love me!" I'm really crying now.

Mom hugs me. "That's a lot of stuff," she says. "I

think I'm going to have to charge you for a double session." She smiles.

I try to smile, but my nose is running and my eyes are puffy. "Mom, am I having a nervous breakdown?"

She laughs. "No. You're just overwhelmed. You've had a lot to deal with lately. Try to let go of all this stuff. Stop carrying it around with you. It's too much," she says gently.

I wipe a hand across my wet face. I don't know how to let go. I have never known how to let go.

"Why don't you go take a bath, put on your pj's, and I'll order pizza?" Mom suggests. "And you can have anything you want on it. Even sausage."

"Okay," I say weakly.

The bath helps. I settle into the couch, wearing my favorite pajamas. I feel warm and toasty. Mom and I eat pizza (half ricotta and spinach, half pepperoni and sausage) and I feel even better. I put my head on her shoulder.

"So what's going on with Chelsea?" Mom asks.

"She's a dictator, a nut case."

"Don't say 'nut case,'" Mom says.

"We started this club, the Mona Lisas, and she's the president. But she's more like a tyrant."

"The Mona Lisas?" Mom says. "What a great name!"

"Mona Lisas and Mad Hatters," we both say, laughing. Our favorite song.

"But anyway, Chelsea has been more like a mad hatter than a Mona Lisa lately. She acts like she's queen of the world or something."

"That doesn't sound like Chelsea. Maybe something's going on with her."

"Yeah. She wants to run the world! I don't even like her anymore, and she's my best friend!"

"Well, don't give up on her yet," Mom says. Then she gets quiet, and I know what's coming. "Alyssa, your dad *does* love you. He's just a very, very selfish man. Many men are. Women, too. It's the culture. Everyone wants what they want when they want it and they don't care who they hurt to get it. And then when they get it, they find out that it wasn't so great after all. It was the dreaming that was so good, not the getting. Do you know what I mean?"

"I guess."

"A year after your father left for L.A., he said he'd made a mistake. He said he missed you and wanted to come back home."

"And you said no?"

"He only wanted to come home because his girlfriend dumped him, and I was easy and comfortable and familiar and he knew what he was getting. He loves you, but he doesn't love me."

She stares off into space, strokes my hair. "And I wasn't the same person anymore. I was stronger. I had thoughts of my own and was starting to dream for the first time in years."

She sighs. "Now don't get me wrong, if he had loved me, I would have taken him back. But he didn't. Eventually he would have left again and that would not have been good for you. And we're doing fine on our own, right?"

"Yeah, but . . . I'm so mad at him!"

"I know, honey. But you've got to forgive him, or it will eat you alive."

I fold my arm across my chest and look away.

"Would you rather be depressed?"

"No, I'd rather be happy and have him punished, too."

Mom laughs. "Boy, do I understand that. But unfortunately, you can't have both. You can either stay angry and be depressed or forgive him and be happy. It's up to you."

"Okay," I say, but really I hope the feelings will just go away by themselves.

"Good. Feel better?"

"I guess." I sink back into her shoulder again. "Well, except for the vegetarian thing."

"Well, why don't we compromise?" Mom says. "How about Tuesdays and Thursdays you pick out what you want for dinner. It doesn't even have to be healthy. McDonald's if you want. I'll make sure you eat right the rest of the week," she says, smiling.

"Okay," I say. I'm getting so tired. Talking about my dad makes me feel tired.

"Now, what's this about Hayden sending you a love note?" Mom asks.

18

THE TRUTH ABOUT HAYDEN

Dillon is standing at my locker. I reach past him and open it into his back. Oops.

"Alyssa, I want to get back together."

"I didn't know we'd broken up."

"Well, I heard you broke up with me," he says, whispering so no one will hear.

"Well, it wasn't, like, official or anything."

"Well, I want to go out again."

"Why, so you can snap my bra?"

The bell rings. I wait a minute, torture him a little. "The thing is, Dillon, you are *really* immature," I say, then give him a little wave (see ya!) and walk away.

"You really think you're something, don't you?" he yells after me.

Mr. Carter seems to be in a particularly happy mood today. "I'm happy to say that we have had our first winners of the homework passes!"

Everyone looks around like the winners have big *W*'s on their heads.

"And the homework passes go to . . ." Mr. Carter does a drumroll on his desk.

"Alyssa Fontana and David Hayes!" I turn bright red. Not only have I been singled out, but I've been singled out with Weezer!

"Would either of you like to read your paragraphs to the class?"

"No!" I shout, remembering what I'd written.

"No!" Weezer says. I can just imagine what he wrote.

"Funny," Mr. Carter says. "Your paragraphs were remarkably similar."

Gee, I wonder why.

I hear giggling. Is that Hayden laughing?

Everyone starts chanting, "Weezer! Weezer! Weezer!" and clapping. I'm not sure whether they are congratulating him or making fun of him.

"All right, everyone calm down. I just wanted you all to know you can do this," Mr. Carter says, handing us the homework passes. "Congratulations, Alyssa and David."

"All right, next assignment. Take out a blank piece of paper." Mr. Carter hands out dictionaries. "We're going to do something different today."

"Uh-oh," Breadman says.

"I'm so proud of you guys, I'm going to let you pick out the words for the next spelling/vocabulary test," Mr. Carter says. "I want each one of you to write down five words you think should be on the test. I will grade this, so don't pick words that are too easy. One word should be much harder than the rest.

"Then I want you to look up the words in the dictionary. Write the dictionary's definition down next to the word, then put your definition down next to the word, in your own words. I will pick the words from your lists for the next test."

We groan. I don't know why, we just do. That's what sixth graders do when we get a new assignment: groan.

I groan out of habit, even though I live for this stuff. I love words.

I grab a dictionary and, starting with the *A*'s, flip around until I find interesting words, words like "agitate," "alienate," "humiliate," and "infuriate." My hard word is "acquiesce." I write out the definitions.

Gee, that didn't take long. I hand my paper in and look around the room. Half the class is staring into space, the other half is flipping through the dictionary looking *agitated*.

Elizabeth F-H seems to be stuck altogether. She hasn't

written one word down. But not Breadman. I look at his list:

1. Focaccia

"You can't put your last name on the spelling test!" I say.

"Why not? No one can spell it! And at least I'll get one right!"

2. Feta

"You are obsessed with food, Breadman."

3. Fungus

"You are so gross!"

4. Fetish

"Eww!"

5. Fiend

"I don't think those are hard enough, Breadman."

"They are for me!"

I wonder what Hayden's words are. "Tormenter"? "Teaser"? "Bully"?

"If you finish early, write in your journal," Mr. Carter says.

I suppose that was for my benefit. So I write:

Dear Gabbie,
I talked about things with Mom last night. It was good. She understood things a lot better than I thought she would.

Elizabeth F-H leans over and whispers in my ear. "Alyssa, I can't think of anything. I don't know what to put."

"It's easy. Just think of people you know," I say. I grab my dictionary and start flipping around again. I suggest some words but don't tell her who I'm thinking of.

"Here, how about 'prima donna' (Chelsea), 'immature' (Dillon), 'cynical' (Bri), 'handsome' (Mr. Carter), and 'malicious' (Hayden)? That's your hard word. It means someone is mean," I explain.

I write a little more in my journal, and then the bell rings.

"Alyssa, can I speak with you a minute?" Mr. Carter asks.

Uh-oh.

"I was looking over your spelling words. Are you all right?" Mr. Carter asks.

"Uh . . ."

"You've seemed a little *agitated* lately," he says, reading from my paper.

"Well, uh, Mr. Carter, did you notice anything . . . um, interesting . . . in my journal?" I ask.

"I just flipped through it. I didn't read it."

"I know, but did anything . . . um . . . jump out at you while you were flipping?"

He laughs, but doesn't say anything.

I have to know. "I was afraid you saw something I wrote about you in my journal."

"Was it good?" he says, laughing again.

"Well, it depends on what you mean by good," I say, blushing.

"Don't worry so much about things. Relax."

"Yeah, I have trouble with that," I say.

"It's easier said than done," Mr. Carter agrees.

"Mr. Carter?"

"Yes, Ms. Fontana?"

"I think you're really cool." I try to look him in the eyes, but I end up looking at the floor.

"Well, I think you're really cool, too," he says.

As I walk toward my locker, I see something sticking out of it. A paper. Not again.

I pull it out. It's a piece of notebook paper with a heart drawn on it. Inside it says "Alyssa & Weezer."

That's it! I've had it. "Alyssa & Weezer" on the desks. "Alyssa & Weezer" notes. I march down to Hayden's locker, where she's getting books out. I push her into her locker. I can't stand being a wimp anymore.

"Wh-what?" she says.

"I've had enough of you and your tricks," I say.

"What do you mean?" Frizzhead asks, looking me straight in the eye. Boy, she's good.

"The love notes, pepperoni, Popsicle sticks—"

"What are you talking about?" she says, straightening up.

"Yeah, right, Hayden," I say, and am about to push her back down again when I hear someone yelling "Weezer! Weezer!" and laughing.

I turn around. It's Dillon! Dillon and Zack O'Brien.

"How's loverboy?" Dillon yells down the hall.

I have a sinking feeling in my stomach. Oh, no. "Hayden . . . uh . . . I might have made a mistake," I say. "I'll be right back. Don't leave." I run down the hall after Dillon.

It's not hard for me to catch up to him, since he's standing in the hall doubled over laughing.

I push him up against the lockers. I am, after all, bigger than he is.

"Whoa!" Zack says, backing away, hands up. "Tomorrow, Dil!"

"Did you put that note in my locker?" I ask, scrunching Dillon's shirt between my fingers.

"What note?"

"Dillon!" I push him harder.

"Well, he seems more your type," he says.

I'm shocked. It *was* him. The Mona Lisas were right.

I let go of his shirt. "And the pepperoni and the Popsicle sticks and all the rest?"

"Yeah, that was Zack's idea."

"Why? Why would you do that? You were supposed to be my friend!"

"You dumped me!"

I make an *L* with my fingers on the top of my head and walk away. *Loser.*

I walk back to Hayden, who is looking at me like I'm a *lunatic.*

"Hayden, I'm so sorry I pushed you. Dillon's been playing tricks on me, but I thought it was you."

She nods. "Well, I wasn't so nice to you when I first came here. I was"—she looks down, embarrassed—"jealous of you. I thought you had the perfect life."

Funny, so did I.

"Until the day I came to your house and found out your dad left, too."

19

THE TRUTH ABOUT CHELSEA

I decide to take a bath, and try to relax, like Mr. Carter said. I light a candle and sink into the water until it's up to my chin. I swirl the water around with my toes, watch the flame flicker on the surface.

I keep hearing Hayden's words in my head over and over. I want to smash something. Will these bad feelings ever go away?

And then I hear it. Faintly, in the back of my mind. "The Tuck-in Song." The sparrow song.

He knows. He cares.

I get out and put on my favorite pants.

"Feeling better?" Mom asks, as I head for my room.

"Yeah," I say. "How was your day?"

Mom looks shocked. Guess I haven't asked in a while. "Good. My day was good, thank you for asking."

I turn back toward my room. I want to write in my journal.

"Lyss?" Mom says hesitantly.

Uh-oh. I hear bad news in her voice.

"I've got to tell you something," Mom says, standing in my doorway. "I spoke to Bri's mom today. She told me the Gardners separated a while ago."

"What!" I sit down slowly on the bed. Not the Gardners—the perfect family!

I think of Mrs. G. in her apron. Meatloaf in the oven. Potatoes. Homemade afghans on the couch. Private riding lessons. Luncheons upstate. Ballet lessons. Chelsea.

"Maybe that's why Chelsea's been acting so weird?" Mom says.

"I guess," I say, dazed. I'm seeing Mrs. G. iron while she watches *Oprah*.

"What happened?"

"I don't know," Mom says.

"I can't believe it."

"Yeah, they seemed to have the perfect life."

I don't feel so bad now. Even the shrink thought so.

"What should I do, Mom? I've been kind of mean to her lately."

"Just be a friend, Alyssa. Why don't you call her up and see if you can stop by sometime?"

When I stop by the next day after school, I think I must have the wrong house. Rock music is blasting through the windows, and someone is singing really loud!

I ring the doorbell and almost fall over when Mrs. G. opens the door. Her hair is really short and sticking out all over. I can't figure out whether that's the style or she's been sleeping on it. And she's wearing jeans and a T-shirt!

"Hi, Alyssa!" she says, smiling. Well, she seems cheerful!

"Hey, Mrs. G.," I say, trying to act like I always do, which is difficult, considering that the place is a total mess. Empty soda bottles and pizza cartons are strewn all over the place. Sections of newspaper cover the floors. And the magazines! Magazines everywhere. I almost slip on one as I make my way to Chelsea's room.

"Chels is in her room," Mrs. G. says. She flops on the couch with a magazine.

Whoa. I've never even seen her sit down before!

Chelsea's room is a mess, too.

"I didn't know," I say.

"I know," she says.

And then Mrs. G. is singing again, at the top of her lungs, some song about someone shattering the illusion of love.

"What is she singing?" I ask.

* 113 *

"One of her favorite songs from high school. She says it's 'cathartic.'" Chelsea rolls her eyeballs. "What does that mean?"

"I think it means she's getting something out of her system," I say, thankful for once that my mom is a shrink.

"Well, I hope she gets it out soon. She's been singing it over and over and over," Chelsea says.

"Maybe she's trying to find herself."

"Well, I hope she finds her old cooking and cleaning self soon."

"Are you okay?"

She nods. "They've been fighting for a long time. It's not like I'm surprised."

"Wow. I can't believe it!"

"And my dad has been coming home really late for a while. Said he was working late."

"But he wasn't?"

"I don't know," she says. "I don't want to know, ya know?"

Yeah, I knew. And then I realized. This was why Chelsea ignored me when I wanted to tell her about my problems. She had enough of her own.

"Are they going to get divorced?"

"I don't know," Chelsea says, looking away.

"Is your mom going to get a job?" I ask.

"I think so. I think she wants to. She yelled at my father that all she did was cook and clean and iron his shirts like she was his maid or something. She never minded when he was home and he was nice to her. But when he started coming home late and had barely anything to say to her, she started to feel like nothing but a servant. They had a big fight about it one night. Woke me up!

"And now that I'm older, it's not like she really needs to be here all day long," Chelsea says, staring off into space.

"Do you see your dad?"

"Every other weekend. He's got an apartment in the city. I still can't believe it."

Me, either.

"My mom wants me to see a counselor."

I don't know what to say. I want to help, but I don't know if I can.

"Lyss?" Chelsea's eyes are full of tears.

"What?" I want to put my arm around her, but I'm afraid to.

"I feel so alone," she says, and then she starts crying really hard.

And so I put my arm around her. And tell her about sparrows.

20

THE MEANEST GIRL

The last few months have been crazy! I can't believe how much has happened.

Hayden Martin, *the meanest girl in school,* comes to my house and tells Mom that her dad left. I find out my father left, too, and is alive, when all this time, I thought he had been killed in an accident on the BQE!

I buy my first bra, and then Mom and I go to the Hard Rock Café, where she actually flirts with the hunky bartender. I didn't think she even noticed guys! Bad thought: Mom having boyfriends.

Chelsea starts the Mona Lisas club so she can be in charge of something, since her life is spinning out of control. We don't do anything except wear red shirts and black jeans, not like Trixie Belden and the Bob-Whites, who always did cool things like solve mysteries and stuff.

I get so stressed over everything that I actually go to

church. And I remember the song Mom used to sing to me about the sparrow and how God is watching over me, a sign that I should just chill out.

Which, of course, I don't.

Especially when someone puts a love note in my locker. I hope it's from someone cute, like Jason Andrews or Mr. Carter. I get all dressed up and it turns out to be Weezer. Weezer! Argh!

Except he didn't write the note. I think it was Hayden, but it turns out to be from Dillon, who is mad at me for breaking up with him, when I didn't even break up with him officially! I almost beat up Hayden thinking she'd done it!

Turns out Hayden was jealous of me because she thought I had the perfect life. I've always thought Chelsea had the perfect life, but it turns out things were really bad at the Gardners' and I never even knew it.

Nicole is standing at my locker when I get to school. I'm so happy to see her.

I barely get "What's up, Nick?" out of my mouth when she says, "I feel so bad. I feel so bad, Alyssa. I just found out about the Gardners."

"Oh, I know. I feel bad, too."

"We were kind of mean to Chelsea at the last meeting," she says.

"I know," I sigh. And then it hits me. *I was mean. Me!* I've never thought of myself as being a mean person before, only other people.

I was the meanest. *The meanest girl.*

"Well, we didn't know. And she *was* acting like a jerk," I say in my defense.

"Well, what are we going to do?" Nicole asks.

"About what?"

"About the Mona Lisas!"

"I don't know!"

"But I still want to be in the club. It was the first time I ever felt part of something!" Nicole looks like she's going to cry.

"But the club is stupid! We never do anything!"

"Well, I talked to Bri and Kei, and they still want to be in it."

The bell rings.

"I'll think about it, Nick," I say.

"TTFN," she whispers to me.

"TTFN," I say, and it doesn't seem so stupid this time.

As I walk down the hall to social studies, I think about what Nicole said about the club, about how everyone still wants to be in it. But why? We don't do anything!

But deep down I know why the club is important. We are there for each other, through good times and bad. And maybe someday we'll be there for other people, too.

As soon as I get to class, I slip Chelsea a note: *Mona Lisas Wednesday night?*

She looks like she will cry from gratitude. "Okay," she writes back.

"Your house?"

"My house," she writes back. "Maybe it will get my mom to clean up!"

After school I stop by Hayden's locker. I'm about to slip something through the slits at the top, when she grabs my hand.

"What's that?" she asks.

Snagged. "Uh . . . an invitation."

"To what?"

To what. Good question. How do I explain the Mona Lisas?

"Have you ever heard of Trixie Belden?" I ask, doubting she has, since no one else I know has ever heard of the books.

"And the Bob-Whites of the Glen? Sure!" Hayden says.

"Trixie and Honey," I say.

"Marty and Di," Hayden says.

"And Jim!" we both say, agreeing that he's the cutest one.

I hand her the invitation.

"I guess we could be like Trixie and Honey," I say, trying to make up for all that has happened.

"Awesome," she says.

"Perfect," I say.

And it is.

Well, almost.